Miracle's Journey

Book Two of the California Dreaming Series

Miracle's Journey

Book Two of the California Dreaming Series

For more information on my upcoming projects, please go to my website: **www.rodneylamarr.com**

Make sure you write a review wherever you purchased this book.

Trigger Warning

This book contains sensitive material about death, trauma, domestic abuse, sexual assault, and violence. If these topics offend you, please do not continue reading this book. I appreciate you supporting my book, but your mental health is more important.

Table of Contents

CHAPTER 1

AFTER THE TRIAL – PT. ONE

THE LINGERING ANGER BURST out, no longer able to be confined within my flesh. With storm clouds of emotion hanging over me, I exploded in every way imaginable. Unfortunately, my room suffered the brunt of my outrage, while the actual target was never phased.

"It looked like Dre was aiming it at the officers." Her words echoed in my mind.

"It looked like Dre was aiming it at the officers."

I sat at the edge of my bed, staring at the blank wall. My poster lay curled on the floor, along with the other wreckage from my outburst. A gentle tap arose from the door.

"You, okay?" my dad asked. His sunken bloodshot eyes highlighted his tiredness. I'm sure I didn't look any better.

He took a step in and paused. His eyes bounced from the books scattered on the floor to the clothes thrown throughout my room. Then he peered over to the flipped trash can perched on my pink chair.

"I'm going to take this," he said, pointing to the disarray in my room, "as a no."

I nodded but didn't look up.

My body shifted slightly as he sat next to me. He placed his forearms against his thighs and leaned forward, matching my posture.

There was a calm silence between us, neither saying a word, just being in each other's presence. That was what I needed. I didn't want him to give me an encouraging speech. I didn't want him to say the cops who killed my brother would get what was coming to them. I just needed someone to be with me.

Unfortunately, the two people I would usually turn to were gone. Dre was dead, and there was nothing I could do to bring him back. And, well, Kim was alive and well. But to me, she was just as gone as Dre.

"I'm so sorry," he said, barely above a whisper. "Come on, let's get you out of this room and get some fresh air."

I followed him into the kitchen. My mom was sitting at the table, looking like a statued version of herself. Her eyes glazed over. Her expression was blank. A trembling hand covered her chapped lips as she stared into the distance. Even her posture seemed to lack life. She was officially a shell of her former self.

My dad walked around her, leaning down to hug her from behind, but she didn't respond. She just sat there like a lifeless corpse. He rubbed her shoulder and kissed the top of her head.

"Want some food?" he asked.

I nodded. Food was the last thing on my mind, although my grumbling stomach would disagree.

"You need to eat something, Bubble Gum. Hell, we all do," he said.

I turned my attention to my mom. Stretching my arm across the table, I placed my hand on hers and squeezed. Dre had been gone for almost six months and her condition had worsened. The trial took her over the edge.

"Mom," I whispered. There was no response. Her gaunt appearance said it all.

Mom and Dre were always close. I guess they were the ying to me and my dad's yang. It was probably because he was her firstborn. Moms always seem to cherish their firstborns more. She loved me too, but it was different. Dre would always be her baby.

"Um…maybe we should order out," my dad said, peering into the refrigerator. "I guess we forgot to go grocery shopping with the trial and everything. Who wants Chinese?" he asked, pushing the refrigerator doors closed. The empty racks intensified the sound of the doors closing, causing the doors to slam.

Mom jerked up; her eyes went wide.

"It's okay, mom," I said, petting her hand.

"Are you ever going to get your phone? It's been buzzing all day. It's driving me crazy. I keep thinking there's a bee in here and you know I don't do bees." My dad cracked a half-smile.

I picked at the General Tso's chicken, moving around the pieces in the small black dish.

"I don't feel like talking to anyone," I said.

"No. We are not doing this again," he said.

"Doing what?" I asked, still looking down at my food.

"We are not hiding in our rooms, shutting the world out. This family has been through enough and Dre wouldn't want us to stop living because," he paused, pressing his lips in a straight grimace. Even the strongest among us didn't have the stomach to admit Dre was dead.

He finally finished with, "Do you understand?"

I sighed but nodded. He turned to my mom and placed his hand over hers.

"Babes?"

She tilted her head up from her untouched meal and glared. Eventually, she mumbled, "okay."

"We *have to* keep going. We have to." There was pain in his voice behind the strength. That is when I realized I had to be strong, not just for Dre but for my dad.

CHAPTER 2

AFTER THE TRIAL – PT. TWO

AFTER DINNER, I RETREATED to my room and straightened up. The posters were placed back on the wall and the trash found a better home in the trash bin. I even vacuumed, which I hated to do.

Afterward, I hopped in the shower, letting the hot, burning water slam against my skin. Even though it was mid-afternoon, I put a pair of pajamas on and slid into my bed.

Thoughts swirled in my head as my eyes scanned my room. Almost every item reminded me of Dre.

A worn stuffed reindeer with a red scarf wrapped around its neck leaned against my bookshelf. Dre had won it for me at Circus Circus in Las Vegas after competing in a basketball tournament. I named him Huey since I loved the Boondocks.

Of course, my parents wouldn't let me watch the show, but Dre filled me in on every episode when my parents weren't around. Eventually, I watched every season and even though they were hilarious, I preferred Dre's retellings more.

An old CD player was next to my laptop, which held the Get Rich or Die Trying CD. This was the first CD I ever owned, which I begged my parents for since Dre told me I "had to" have it.

Despite not being for "impressionable minds," as my dad put it, he allowed it. But if he heard any cursing coming out of my mouth, Dre and I would be in trouble. I never said any cursing…well, not in front of my dad anyways.

My smile soon vanished as my eyes moved to a picture frame on my nightstand. In the background, giant lettering read Santa Monica stretched along the wall. Beautiful colors illuminated the painted palm trees and ocean skyline within the letters.

Three smiling kids posed in front of the wall, embracing as siblings should. I was in the middle. Dre was on my left and then there was Kim to my right.

My anger resurfaced as I pressed my hand against my desk for support. I slammed the picture frame down. I couldn't look at her face right now. Too many emotions were running in my head and I was afraid some of those emotions would creep out. No one would want that. Not right now.

I reached for my cell phone and scrolled through the music until I found the right song; Kanye West's *Black Skinhead*. I gently slid my headphones over my braids, finding their usual resting spot.

As the tribal beat began, I closed my eyes and allowed the music to take over. My shoulders slumped as my back pressed against the headboard. My head instantly danced to the beat. I sang along.

> *"For my theme song*
> *My leather black jeans on*
> *My by any means on*
> *Pardon, I'm getting my scream on…."*

Suddenly a familiar sensation rushed over me. Goosebumps covered my arms and it felt like my body was no longer under my control. The darkness grew as my soul plummeted into an open abyss; for once, this feeling felt freeing.

Darkness.

CHAPTER 3

AFTER THE TRIAL –PT. THREE

AMID THE DARKNESS, AN unfamiliar banging reverberated against my inner self, sending chills down my spine. The sound grew stronger while my soul sank further and further into the still void.

The darkness soon vanished as the world became alive once more. The sun's brightness shined from above while my toes pressed against the sand. An intoxicating smell of the ocean flowed through the air as water sprinkled along my cheeks.

When my eyes regained focus, I stood staring at a vast ocean, waves crashing against the beach, warning others of Mother Nature's true power.

A group of men and women stood aligned next to me. The shaved heads of the men reflected the sun's brightness. Circular plates filled their ear lobes as some adorned battle scars, lining their half-naked bodies.

The women were not much different. Cloth skirts wrapped around their waists. Beaded necklaces hung over their chest, acting as their only source of coverage. They looked upon the horizon, scowls adorning their faces.

I turned to the ocean and stared, trying to find the reason for their inquisitive expressions. In the far distance, a ship emerged amongst the waves. And then another. There must have been at least a dozen ships heading towards us.

The large wooden ships continued their path, swaying against the violent waves. Two large t-shaped poles extended from the main decks. Ropes kept them secure.

Gasps emerged from the people alongside me. Shouting and laughter arose from behind us. I turned to find another group of men staring out into the ocean. Smiles crossed their faces.

They spoke, but their words were foreign to me.

"*Hepe Kuni moli*," a man screamed.

The men gripped long wooden staffs that they pounded into the sand. With every pound came a monstrous bang.

The young man beside me turned and sprinted in the opposite direction, kicking up sand in my face; more gasps from my group. The man made it maybe 20 yards until a spear plunged into his shoulder, sending his body collapsing to the ground.

A handful of men ran to him. Their feet collided with his body, stomping him ruthlessly. Pleads of what I assumed were mercy rang out from the people alongside me, but they went unanswered.

"*Hunge anatusado,*" a woman screamed.

"*Tefadhalo acha. Hunge,*" a man pleaded.

A man stepped forward from the other group. Bamboo-like sticks pierced his nose as his skinny fingers danced in the air. His gruff voice commanded attention.

"*Kotoshia,*" he yelled.

The others corrected their behavior and slowly raised the battered man to his feet. They shoved him forward and he collapsed in front of me.

Men from my line lunged forward, grabbing him from the ground. They wrapped their arms around him, steadying his wobbly knees. Blood dripped from his face.

I clenched my fist but knew better than to say or do anything. I learned from previous "episodes" that maybe I was just supposed to watch. Learn from history's cruelty.

The leader scowled as he peered at his opponents.

"*Kowi magoti yeki.*" He slammed his staff into the dirt and my group fell to their knees. I did the same. Another command rang out and my group turned to the approaching vessels.

The large ships were positioned maybe 200 yards away from the beach as little boats were dropped from their sides. The boats slammed against the ship as waves threw them like rag dolls.

My eyes shut as I prayed that this "episode" would end soon. I dreaded the harsh reality that would quickly come to life. When my eyes opened, the small boats were now rowing forward, heading straight towards us.

The lady beside me cried out, but her screams didn't exist alone. Soon, more cries roared through the air as tears rolled down the cheeks of my fellow captives. I turned to face the leader of the other group.

A large toothless smile spread across his face. Pleasure poured out of his eyes as the small boats approached. When I turned back, the boats were onshore and armed men were walking toward us. They dragged large ropes over their shoulders, which already had weapons resting on them.

The first was an older man, pulled from his knees and tied; first his hands, then his neck. My heart burst from my chest as anger poured over every inch of me.

A young woman screeched out as the men forced her inside a boat. Her screams were met with a slap to the face and a few chuckles from the captors. This was fun for them.

More and more men and women were loaded onto the boats. Due to the overcrowding, they nearly sat on top of each other. My eyes scanned the scene as an armed man approached me. I stood up and met his eyes.

I wanted to show him I wasn't afraid of him, but the look he gave me made me shutter. It was the look someone gave someone or something with no value.

As he tightened the rope around my neck, I saw the other group's leader wrap his arms around knives and swords, prizes for his cooperation, no doubt. He waved his newfound treasure in the air as his men cheered in delight.

"Oshinadi! Oshinadi! Oshinadi!" they screamed.

With a slight tug of the rope, my body wrenched forward, resulting in an uncontrollable gasp. With every step, a piece of my soul died.

Two men held the boat steady as I stepped inside. My feet sank into two feet of ice-cold water. My body shivered and my breathing slowed. I wrapped my arms around myself for warmth. When my butt felt the wooden seat, I fell forward and my soul sank again.

The boat's rocking became no more and was replaced by the exhilarating feeling of falling. The darkness came alive, reaching for me, taking me away to a safer place.

CHAPTER 4

TODAY

THE ENTICING SMELL OF bacon woke my senses as my eyes flung open. The new day's sun shined in between the window blinds, illuminating my room. I sprung up with purpose and headed straight to the kitchen.

Before making it down the hallway, a piercing sound rang in the air. I turned the corner to see my dad scrambling around the kitchen. My eyes widened as he twirled a dish towel in the air, trying to disperse the black smoke from encircling the smoke alarm.

With his bare hand, he grabbed the pot and instantly regretted it.

"Hot hot hot," he shouted, sliding the flaming hot dish onto the counter, grease splattering everywhere. Steam bellowed from the pan as the unmistakable smell of grease blanketed the kitchen.

The microwave chirped its own sound, adding to my dad's hectic cooking strategy. I stood in the doorway, speechless, unsure how to help. So, I just stared as my dad flailed around, trying to tame this chaotic scene.

When the kitchen returned to its usual silence, my dad leaned over the counter, head hung low, panting.

"What's going on?" I asked.

"I was trying to make you breakfast."

"I can see that," I said. "Did it work?"

He raised his head and simply nodded.

CHAPTER 5

AFTER A DELICIOUS BOWL of Fruit Loops, I showered and headed to the living room.

"Did you finish all your homework for the weekend?"

"Yes, Sir," I said. "Did *you* do all of *your homework*, Daddie-O?"

He looked up from the laptop, eyebrows raised and face perplexed. He shrugged.

"This math stuff wasn't this hard when I was in school. Why the heck do I need to take math anyways?"

"I'm pretty sure you need math in leadership."

"It's Business Administration and I thought all I had to do was read and write. Not math," he said, staring back at his laptop. I laughed.

A slight tap on the front door startled us. When he opened the door, a surprising voice emerged from the hallway.

"Hey, Clyde."

He opened the door wider.

"Mom? What are you doing here?"

"Well, I figured you could use some help. Raising a kid on your own isn't easy, baby."

"I'm not raising her alone, mom," my dad said.

"And, baby, I'm so sorry about Andre. I loved that boy like he was my own," she said, pushing my dad out the way as she stepped inside.

"Hey, Madea!" I wrapped my arms around her, almost breaking her frail body.

"Hey, Bubble Gum. How's my favorite granddaughter?"

"I'm your only granddaughter, Madea," I said.

"Spitting image of ya momma, you sure is." She cupped my cheeks, "but I see ya daddy in ya eyes." I returned her observation with a cheek-squished smile.

After letting my cheeks go, I helped her with her bags and walked her to the living room.

"Are you staying with us, Madea?" I asked.

"Of course, Bubble Gum," she said.

"You sure, mom? I can pay for a hotel. We don't really have…," my dad began but was quickly cut down by Madea's motherly glare.

"You trying to get rid of me, already? I'm staying. This is where you need help. Not at some hoddy toddy hotel, boy. Now go put my bags in Miracle's room," she commanded.

"My room? Um, where am I going to sleep?"

"We can sleep in the same room, child. I'm a buck 50 when wet. I don't take much room. You won't even notice I'm there."

I glanced at my dad.

"Uh…I'll get your bags, Mom."

My eyes followed my dad as he grabbed a big flowered suitcase and dragged it into the hallway. He peered back at me and shrugged while mouthing the words, "I'm sorry." I shook my head and frowned.

When I turned back to Madea, I caught her studying me. Her expression was somber and a glimpse of worry was written all over her face.

"How you doing, baby? You okay?" she asked in a grandmotherly-like way.

My head lowered and I fidgeted with my fingers.

"I'm fine." I didn't look up.

Her hand reached my chin and lifted my head, making me meet her eyes.

"How you really doing, child, and don't tell me no B.S. I'm ya grandma. I can tell when ya lying."

"Madea, I promise. I'm fine."

Her eyes locked on mine. She stared for a few moments, reading my expression.

"Okay, baby girl. If you say so." She turned to walk away but stopped. "But you know, Madea always knows the truth. Always." With that, she headed into the hallway to "our" room.

CHAPTER 6

LATER THAT NIGHT, I rolled the sleeping bag onto my bedroom floor. This wasn't how I expected to spend the last week of school before summer break, but I never really had a choice.

My bathroom door opened and Madea slid out. Her straight hair converted into a trailer park of pink curlers. Her faded nightgown went down to her skinny ankles and reminded me of a large potato sack...only covered with green and yellow flowers.

The distinct smell of vapor rub engulfed the room, forcing my nose to scrunch up with every breath. She looked around. Sliding open the nightstand, she reached in and pulled out a faced-down picture frame, examining it. Her eyes shot up at me and then back at the image.

She adjusted the picture frame to face the bed. Slipping her hand into her bag, she pulled out a black and white image of two girls, arm in arm. Smiles decorated their faces. She kissed the image and slid the picture over mine.

"Is that you?" I asked.

"Sho is, child. And this right here," she said, pointing to the girl on the left, "is my sister."

"Aunt Thelma?"

"Child, Thelma was 300lbs since birth. This ain't no Thelma." I smiled. "This right here is your Great Aunt Dorothy. We called her Dot Jean."

"She gone too?" I asked. I couldn't keep up with her siblings. She had like 6 or 7 brothers and sisters. Most people her age did. I guess that's the price you pay for not having the internet or TV to keep you busy.

"Yeah, she's gone too," Madea said.

She reached into her bag, grabbed a large white box, placed it on the nightstand and climbed into the bed. Tubes flowed out of the box and I thought I heard water swishing from inside the device. With a flip of a switch, the machine came alive with the sounds of mini wind storms emerging from the face mask at the end of the tube.

"What the hell is that," I thought. But my words were more respectful when they left my mouth.

"Madea, what is that?"

"Oh, that's my CPAP, baby. I can't breathe when I sleep without it."

I sighed.

"But don't worry, Bubble Gum, you won't even notice it's on."

The neon glow of the clock read 2:45. The fast-puffing air echoed throughout the room like rhythmic balloons inflating. I looked over at Madea.

Her petite frame was stretched out on my very comfortable bed. Her left eye was slightly ajar as if she was staring at me in her sleep. Creepy!

I turned my head and stared at the ceiling. My back ached from the hard floor. My eyes felt like desert sand and my tired soul yearned for quiet.

I gathered my stuff and slowly tiptoed out of the room, pausing at every creek of the floor.

I slid Dre's door open slowly to not disturb the ghosts that may live inside. It was the first time I went into his room since, well, you know. It was the first time anyone had been inside Dre's bedroom.

I exhaled deeply and stared. Even after more than a year, his faint smell still lingered. Memories of my brother streamed into my consciousness. From building a fort in the living room with couch cushions as walls to fighting over if I had stolen the candy bars from his room…which usually I did. From first loves to broken hearts. He was always there for me. Always.

My feet danced around a cluster of stuff sprawled across the bedroom floor. I dodged his phone charger and passed the few empty candy wrappers, nearly stubbing my toe on his pair of adjustable dumbbells.

As I sat down on his bed, sinking into his mattress, a tingling spread across my arms. With one long sigh, I leaned back, pressing my head against his pillow. My eyelids sank and I drifted off to sleep.

CHAPTER 7

WILLOW MARIE'S SONG *ABOUT* *Last* *Night* blared from my cell phone, alerting me it was officially 6:30 and a new day had begun. I sat up to my dad, staring at me from the doorway.

"Dad—" I began, but he cut me off with a wave of his hand.

"It's fine, baby girl." He glanced around the room. "I didn't know when someone," he sighed loudly. "When I would be able to come back in here."

He bit his lower lip and examined the room again. His eyes locked on various items but eventually found their way to me.

"You should have been the first one back in here, Miracle. It always should have been you." I returned his comment with a guilty smile.

"Plus, I've had to share a room with my mom, so I get it. Trust me on that. I get it." With that, he patted the door frame and slowly closed the door.

My legs flung over the bed as I did my own examination of the room. I stood up and fingered through a few dust-covered items on his nightstand.

I lifted the Kobe Bryant figurine, praying silently to him and his family. Then, twirling the fidget spinner, I flipped through one of those black journals most kids used during school.

The nightstand drawer was filled with some old school papers and a few unfinished letters. A faced-down picture frame sat underneath a few sheets of paper. Lifting the frame, a smile crossed my face as a picture I had taken appeared.

Dre sat on a school bench. His smile was infectious. His arms wrapped around a girl with long flowing braids. Her chipmunk cheeks highlighted her mesmerizing smile, full of life and emotion. Her hazel eyes gleamed with happiness as she stared into the camera. It was Ashley, or as Dre would put it, "the girl who got away." She was good for him.

"Thought they'd last forever," I mumbled.

After the breakup, he must have been too heartbroken to throw away her picture. I once asked him why they broke up and all he would say was "broken promises." That sounded too complicated for my understanding, but that's what love is: complicated.

My attention turned to his desk, where I found another black notebook, a few pens, and more candy wrappers.

"And this is why I stole your candy, bro," I whispered to the ghost of my memories. After a few more moments to thrive in the past, I got my stuff together and got ready for school.

CHAPTER 8

"HEY, LADY," GREG SAID, leaning against my locker.

I wrapped my arms around him, tilted my head, and pressed my lips against his. He always smelt sweet. I didn't know if it was from his addiction to sugar or just his essence. Either way, I loved it. I mean, I liked it.

"Hey, what's up with you?" I asked.

"Nothing, counting down the days until school is done."

"I know, right? This week is going to take forever," I said.

Our hands interlocked and we proceeded to our usual spot; a bench in the west quad. There wasn't much traffic there, so my people-watching skills became rusty, but I enjoyed the quiet.

This was the first time we walked hand in hand, like for real, boyfriend and girlfriend. I wasn't sure if that was what we were, but I wouldn't hate the thought. Greg was certainly handsome enough.

His pecan brown eyes had a glimmer of gold and his smile could light up the darkest nights. I liked weird things about him, like how he texted and held the door open for me. I knew it was small, but it was sweet. He was sweet.

"What's up with you? You keep checking your phone," I said.

"Nothing." I knew him well enough to know when he was lying. His lip would always curl up this particular way.

"Greg?" I asked.

He sighed.

"My dad texted me the other day. I'm not sure what to do." His eyes focused on the ground while his feet tapped against the pavement.

"Your dad? Thought he was in Florida or something."

"He is. Well, he was. He's coming to Calie for a work thing and wants to see us. Well, the boys anyways." He finally turned to me, a grimace set on his face.

"Oh," I said.

We sat in silence for a moment. A billion questions stirred in my mind. I laced my fingers in his, sinking my fingertips into his soft palms. My head leaned against his shoulder.

"What are you going to do?" I asked.

"No clue. I spent seven years without him. I don't need him. Never have." His words lacked the confidence one would expect, but I let them go.

"What is he like?" I asked.

"No idea. My only memory of him is of the night he walked out."

"Will you tell me about it?"

He turned to me; eyes narrowed.

"Please," I said. "You know everything about me. I think it's time I knew something about you."

"You know me."

"Yeah, I know you're a zombie freak, think robots will take over the world—"

"Which they will," he said, bobbing his head up and down.

"I'm serious. Will you tell me? I mean, if you want to. You don't have to."

He let out a deep sigh and nodded.

"Okay."

He began:

My eyes flung open as the room filled with my mother's screams. I threw my legs over the bed and stared, trying to cast out her pain. Rain tapped danced on the window as thunder roared in the background. The only light was the reflected stars from the twins' pack-and-play.

I pushed myself out of bed and tiptoed to the door. As it crept open, I prayed the usual noises were muted through the storms inside and outside the house. An irritating creek shot out while a low rumble emerged from the depths of their room. I peered down the hall. Another shout rang out.

Their door burst open with my father racing out, two gym bags in hand.

"Where the hell do you think you are going?" my mother screamed, standing in the entryway of their room.

My father stopped as he crossed my path. I stared lovingly into his eyes, but there was discontent staring back. He placed his hand on my shoulder and leaned down.

"You'll have to be the man of the house now. Ya, hear me?"

"Yes, Sir," I said, barely grasping what that meant.

"Don't take crap from anyone, ya hear?" His voice was stern.

"Yes, Sir," I repeated.

An object flew through the air, narrowly missing my father's temple.

"Dammit, Chere. You hit me and then I hit you, got me?" Spit flew from his mouth as his voice echoed in the hallway.

My mother wound up and threw another object. A shoe landed perfectly against my father's shoulder. She charged with reckless abandon. Her arms flailed in the air as her nails scratched away at his skin, piercing his flesh.

He tried to block, pushing his bags between himself and the fiery scorned woman. He slowly backpedaled into the living room, where he countered the attack.

As my mother's right-hand dove to my father's chin, he stepped aside and swung. The blow knocked my mother off her feet, sending her flying through the air.

She slammed down in the middle of the living room, the floor covered in her blood. My father stepped forward to finish her for good. I ran to her, shielding her body as she crouched on the floor.

His eyes met mine and he lowered his fist, calming his posture. His shoulders dropped as he stared at me. I didn't know what I was expecting. Maybe an apology or perhaps a sign of regret. Instead, my father did the last thing I ever expected. He turned around and walked out the door.

I stared at the door for what seemed like hours, waiting for my father to return. But he never did. So, I turned my attention to my mother, who lay on the floor, squirming in pain.

"Mommy, are you okay?" I asked.

She carefully opened and closed her jaw; I assumed to see if it still worked. Her hands shook as her palm kissed her bruised forehead. Her eyes were already starting to swell.

"That son of a," she paused. "I can't believe him. What did I tell you? Men ain't nothing but dogs. Don't you turn out like him, you hear me? Do you hear me?" Her eyes were locked on mine.

"Yes, Ma'am," I stuttered.

"Now, go into the room and check on the twins. I'll be alright. Don't worry about me. I've been hit with harder punches than that." She slowly got onto her elbow, trying to regain her balance.

I stood up and slowly walked to the hallway. I turned back just as she spat a mouthful of blood on the floor. She rotated her head from left to right and caught me in the corner of her eye.

"Boy, I told you to go check on your brothers. Now go, Greg!"

I turned and walked away.

"Dang," I said. "Greg, I'm so sorry. That's messed up." I squeezed his hand harder.

"Yeah." His shoulders slumped and his eyes reddened.

We sat there staring at the ground. My mind questioned a love that would deliberately cause pain to the other. Thoughts of my parents raced in my head. They weren't perfect, especially lately, but I knew they would always love each other, even while separated.

CHAPTER 9

AT LUNCH, GREG AND I stepped out into the courtyard; steam from the pavement greeted us. The blazing sun heated our bodies as the dry air filled our lungs. Beads of sweat instantly dripped from our brows, the joys of a California summer.

In front of us, a girl flailed her arms and turned to shake her butt as her friend followed every movement with her phone. Afterward, they'd hovered over the phone, reviewing every missed beat. They repeated this process several times before embracing in high fives and hugs filled with smiles.

Further down, skateboarders huddled around a table. Apparently, it was too hot for them to master their own tricks, so they watched videos of professionals flipping through the air.

A girl sporting afro-puffs and an Erykah Badu t-shirt sliced between us as her phone blasted Lizzo's song *Good as Hell.*

As she moved past, my body twisted forward and darkness wrapped its arms around me, pulling me into complete emptiness. The warmth of Greg's body next to me was replaced by the cool chill of a dark void.

I awoke with my feet already in motion. My arms stretched out in front of me as hands grasped onto mine. The familiar sound of children singing in unison caught my attention first. The voices boomed in the air, shaking even the steadiest structures.

My eyes open to find myself amongst a parade of children, lined in rows, moving forward with a purpose. Their faces gleamed with happiness and joy as they pressed on.

Along the sidewalk, people gawked at the sight. Some held signs that were not appropriate for the eyes of the youths. Others made their anger felt by taunting and hurling curse words in the kids' direction. But still, they pressed forward.

A man in his mid-30s threw a soda can at one of the kids. His actions weren't met by the other bystanders descending on him; it was met with applause from the crowd.

But it was also met with our voices singing louder than before. His hatred was no match for their innocent love.

I looked down and the most amazing brown eyes I have ever seen stared back at me. It was her. She stared into my eyes as her lips poured a song of power and love, just like the others. As the group's pace slowed, we both looked forward.

A line of police cars and fire trucks stood in front of us. Red and blue sirens flashed before us. With folded arms, the men sneered in our direction. Some even made their presence felt with verbal abuse. One man stepped forward and the others waited for his command.

The children stopped, waiting to see what was to come. The man slowly lifted a bullhorn to his lips and spoke.

"You are in violation of the law. Disperse now, or you will be sent to jail."

The kids turned their heads and looked at each other. Soft murmurs were heard from the crowd. Then, one brave soul yelled, "We shall not be moved!" The kids erupted, screaming a song from the top of their lungs, loud enough for Heaven to hear.

The man's eyebrows rose while his lips pursed. His face turned rose-red as he huffed. His chest expanded, lifting the bullhorn once again.

"I repeat. You are in violation of the law. Disperse now." He paused. "You have until the count of ten. One."

The singing continued.

"Two."

No effect.

"Three. Four.". With every count, the singing grew louder and more powerful. Bystanders smiled with an evil knowledge of what was to come.

"Nine," he shouted. He lowered the bullhorn and turned to one of the firefighters. His command was inaudible from my location, but the fireman grimaced. He shook his head but was met with a harsh reaction from the commander.

What happened next was gut-wrenching. I would not believe the tragic events of that day if I were not present to witness them. On the final count of ten, the firefighters turned their hoses to the small, fragile children.

The water rushed out with such force kids were knocked off their feet. Some flew ten yards away, while the lighter ones, usually the younger ones, went further. Skin peeled off the kids like it was held on by fragile material.

Screams of horror rung out. But these screams … these nightmarish screams didn't just come from the kids. Bystanders watched in horror. I guess they didn't realize what their actions and taunts would lead to.

As I watched in disgust, more water from another hose pierced through the crowd like cannon balls. Kids tried to cover up, but the force was too powerful. I turned to the brown-eyed girl, but she was running for safety, matching the action of others.

She ducked behind a car as police officers approached…their batons at the ready. My feet moved without thought and I ran to her. I was 5 yards away when my body felt a jolt like no other. It kicked me back a few feet as the freezing water engulfed me, knocking the wind out of me.

The pain was unbearable. I tried to cover up, but the force was too powerful. I was stapled to the floor as water became my biggest enemy. Sadly, relief only came when the firefighters targeted another set of children a few feet away from me.

With every strength I had left, I lifted my head to see the officers standing over the brown-eyed girl. Their batons hung in the air as time stood still.

I screamed, "Noooo!" as their weapons crashed into their target.

Then, the world went dark.

CHAPTER 10

MY BODY JERKED FORWARD as I screeched out in pain.

"Miracle, you okay?" Greg asked. He searched my body, checking for any plausible reason why I screamed.

My eyes went wild, searching around me. The sight of him brought me back to reality. I was safe, back at school, back with him.

My eyes clenched shut and my head shot up as I focused on slow breaths.

"What's going on?" he asked. The dancing girls stopped and focused on my erratic behavior. Even Afro-puffs paused for a moment, then proceeded on her way.

"Nothing, sorry. It was um…a bee. And you know I don't do bees," I said.

"Bees?" He twisted his face, probably not buying my corny excuse. "Are you sure you're okay? You're acting weird. Like weirder than normal weird."

I leaned in and whispered, "It's a woman thing. We can talk about it if you want."

His cheeks went flush as his chin dropped.

"No, um… I understand. We're good."

"That should buy me some time," I thought. I hated to use the "it's a woman thing" excuse, but sometimes it comes in handy.

"Yo, I'm open."

"Get him!"

"D up. D up."

The conversation from the ongoing basketball game caught my attention, releasing Greg from his world of embarrassment. I stepped closer to the basketball court. Memories of my brother floated up. Basketball always reminded me of Dre. Hell, almost everything reminded me of him.

"You decide what you're going to do about your dad?" I asked, still staring at the game.

Greg stepped up shoulder to shoulder with me.

"I think I'll see him."

"What? Really? That's good, right?" I asked.

"Not sure. But I'd rather see what happens instead of living with what-ifs, you know?" Greg said.

"How did you become so mature, young man?" I smiled.

"Well, I think it's the company I…" Greg tripped over absolutely nothing before he could finish. His bag flew a few feet away while his lean body sprawled against the blacktop.

"How is this even possible?" I chuckled.

"Miracle."

"I'm just kidding. Don't freak—"

"Miracle. Look." He pointed towards a group of guys huddled against the wall.

Blue handkerchiefs hung from the back pockets of their pants, which barely concealed their worn underwear. Several had tattoos graffitied on their arms, while others chose their necks as the canvas. But the muscular teen in the middle sent my heart racing. It was Rieko.

"Oh my God," I said. My reaction was automatic and I barrelled forward, pulling Greg's arm. He barely had time to recover his things before I yanked him forward.

"Are you sure this is a good idea?" Greg said. His voice was shaky, but I didn't answer or slow my pace.

Rieko's hands waved in the air, pointing his fingers at no one in particular. He paced back and forth in the small circle within the confines of his friends. His head swung from member to member, ensuring each person was addressed.

As we got closer, one of the guys noticed us. He narrowed his eyes and whispered something to the others; they all turned and glared at us. Rieko stopped talking. A frown rested on his lips.

He stepped forward, parting the group. I met him a few feet away from his friends. Greg lagged behind.

"Hey, Miracle. I —"

"Rieko, where have you been?"

"Good to see you too, little girl," he said.

My demeanor softened and I shook my head.

"Sorry, good to see you." He embraced me with a side hug, pulling me into him.

"Yeah, police hemmed me up when they came around asking about Dre. Put me away for a while since they found some things in my pocket. But as you can see, it didn't stick." He waved his arms in the air. "I'm free as a bird now because of a stupid clerical error. I don't know."

"Oh, okay. Congrats. Listen, was it you? Tell me the truth."

His face melted and his tough exterior seemed to soften somehow. His eyes met mine. Then, he tilted his head up and stared into the clouds.

"Listen, I'm sorry about Dre. He was a good dude. He didn't deserve this," Rieko said. The muscles in his arms tensed as veins bulged. "What those cops did to him…you can't come back from that. It's messed up, yo. We can't let that slide."

I wanted to stop him and ask him the question again, but as I looked into his eyes, I saw he was hurting too. People would accept me being angry and sad, but I supposed his tough reputation wouldn't allow him to unveil his mask.

Rieko went silent and continued staring into the heavens. I didn't push him. I looked back at Greg, who held his head down, lost in his thoughts.

"Remember that day Dre was about to get busy with that wonder bread dude?" He asked, still staring into the sky.

"Wonder bread?" I asked.

"The skinhead dude from around the way," he said. "Looks like his face got mauled by a cheese grater or something?"

Erik, I thought.

"Yeah, I remember. What does he have to do with Dre? Do you think he gave it to Dre? That doesn't make sense."

"What? Nah. Not like that. When we went back to my spot, I told Dre that Wonder Bread would probably be gunning for his head. You know your boy, Dre, wasn't dumb. He understood that."

He turned and stared down at me.

"Well, I asked him if he needed…," he looked around to ensure the conversation wasn't overheard, "protection."

"Yeah, and?" I asked.

"He said he already had some. Protection, I mean," Rieko said.

"Wait…he already had it?"

"He already had it." He repeated. "I was just as shocked as you were. Dre wasn't like that at all. He was street, but not street, ya feel me?"

I turned to Greg, who shot me a curious look.

"That doesn't make any sense … then where did he get it?" I asked, turning back to Rieko. Frustration rang in my voice, but I couldn't control that.

"No clue, baby girl. You know I'd tell you if I knew. That's on everything. Dre was family to me." He tapped his hand over his chest.

Greg and I walked away with even more questions than when we started. It didn't make any sense. None of this made any sense.

CHAPTER 11

ON THE FIRST DAY of school, I raced into my classroom, searching for the perfect desk. There were specific requirements my future desk had to meet. First, it had to be next to the window so I could stare aimlessly outside, just in case class was boring.

The second requirement was it had to be in the perfect row. It couldn't be in the front row (I didn't want all the teacher's attention on me) and it couldn't be in the last row. Everyone knew that row was reserved for those who found school to be…let's just say unimportant. Since I actually cared about my grades, that row was out. And the final requirement was it had to be next to my best friend's desk.

That was my thought on the first day of school. After over 175 days of school and a gut-wrenching trial, I groaned at the thought of her mere inches away from me. I guessed this was what happened when your best friend blamed your brother for his own death.

I felt her blue eyes piercing my personal bubble, but I refused to look in her direction. With my arms crossed, I stared at the front of the class, anger boiling inside me. We hadn't spoken since the day of the trial.

My heart shattered every time memories of that day reappeared in my mind: her walking to the witness stand, raising her hand, and swearing to tell the truth and nothing but.

I closed my eyes and took deliberate breaths.

"Calm down," I told myself.

Fortunately, since it was the last week before summer break, most teachers opted to watch movies instead of teaching the students. English class was no different. Mr. Haywood slid in the DVD, and Romeo and Juliet appeared on the SMART board.

While the other students stared at a young Leonardo De Caprio, I pulled over my hood, concealing my face from the world as my earbuds rested in my ears. Willow Marie's soulful voice rang out, singing sweet melodies about a young girl lost in the big city. "Fitting," I thought.

> *"The city lights flash,*
> *The rain does fall,*
> *Strangers zoom by,*
> *Waiting for their call,*
> *This is the life we want,*
> *But does it want us?"*

My body sank into a non-existent ocean of life engulfed in darkness. The class was no more and gravity ceased to exist. As I fell, my soul reached out for any trace of the light, but it was too late. The darkness had already won.

CHAPTER 12

THE GASOLINE SMELL HIT my nose as the familiar sound of a bus taking off rose in the darkness. My eyes slowly opened, bringing about the brightness of the morning sun. Maroon and gold banners hung from the walls as students zoomed past, piling into the building. I didn't understand. I was still at school.

My head jerked left and right, trying to figure out why I was there. Then, I saw him. My mouth hung open while my knees nearly buckled. My heart exploded with pain and sadness then with happiness and joy. My hand flew to my eyes as I wiped away the stinging tears.

"Dre," I whispered.

It was him. My sweet, sweet brother. It took everything inside of me not to go running towards him and wrap my arms around him. Or to tell him not to carry a gun or…So many things raced in my head. Instead, I took a deep breath and resisted.

Dre walked toward a girl who also looked familiar. It was Ashley, his ex-girlfriend. Ashley was pacing back and forth.

I crept closer, ensuring I stayed in the shadows. Hiding behind a half brick wall, I stalked the two star-crossed lovers. Thankfully, they couldn't see me. Ashley was mumbling to herself as Dre approached.

"You can do this. Just breathe. Just do it already," she whispered to herself. Her appearance looked off. Her round cheeks were sunken, matching her now frail appearance. Her hair was unkempt and her baggy clothes were camouflaged in wrinkles. Her hands curled as they pressed against the sides of her head.

"Do what?" Dre asked. She jumped back, startled at his presence. She whipped her button-down sweater closed, wrapping it around her body tightly.

"What?" her voice growled.

Her eyes were dark pools of fear or hate; I couldn't tell. But the emotion was real. Their eyes met, but she quickly broke them off.

"Ash?" Dre stepped closer. "Ash?"

"Dre, don't," she commanded. Her hands flung up, blocking his advance. I leaned forward, hanging on every word.

"Don't what?" Dre shrugged. He took a step back. "What's going on with you? You're acting crazy."

"I'm fine," she said. The vein in her forehead throbbed. Her smile appeared forced. "Just," she waved her hand in the air, then clenched it shut, "just leave me alone."

Her eyes grew wide as her complexion grew white. I followed her field of vision, which led me past the students holding hands, stealing kisses behind the teacher's back and past two kids waving imaginary light-sabers at each other. It led me to two kids in particular.

The two stepped out of a beat-up brown Nissan truck. Five or six air fresheners hung on the rear-view mirror as a man chugged what looked to be a beer. His face was scrunched towards the students as they slammed the door, causing the man to spill his "beer." The man shouted at the older kid, who provided his own physical gestures to who I just assumed was his beloved father. The younger student smiled with glee. Erik!

I turned back to Dre, whose eyes were also locked on Erik and what I assumed was his brother. They shared a square chin and tall, slim builds. Dre turned his attention back to Ashley.

Ashley bit her bottom lip. Her eyes narrowed, blinking rapidly. Her hand slid into her sweater, remaining there for minutes. Mumbles escaped her mouth but were too low for me to hear. Dre moved forward, stopping inches away from her. She jolted backward as if she had just remembered Dre was still there.

"What the hell are you doing?" Dre didn't wait for an answer. He shoved his hand into her sweater. She tried to struggle and that was when his eyes opened wide. Her reaction said it all. Her eyes grew wide, matching his. Dre mouthed her name.

"Let go, Dre," she commanded.

"What the hell, Ash?" Dre looked around and then pushed her around the brick wall. I leaned back to avoid being seen. After a few seconds, I peeked my head around the corner.

"What the hell is this, Ash," he repeated.

"Shut up," she said through gritted teeth. "Get off of me, Dre."

She squirmed around, trying to break his grip. I didn't know if I should run and push him off of her. But maybe that would mess up the timeline or whatever. Dang it. I wished I had paid attention to Greg more when he went on about all his sci-fi movies.

"Ash, stop!" Dre's voice rose higher than I had ever heard. His eyes burned through hers. "Just stop!"

Her eyes met his. Ashley stared at him with hate. I had never seen her give Dre that look before. With that stare, he had to feel like he was two feet tall, but he didn't let go. I clenched my jaw and continued to watch. She didn't budge. Neither did he.

He mouthed the words, "Stop, please."

Her head sank. A soft whimper emerged as tears began to slide down her cheeks.

"Were you going to …" his thoughts cut him off as her reality became his.

"You can't do this. I won't let you, Ash. I won't." His voice found its calm tone. Dre moved one step closer so his body was pressed against hers. His head shot to the left and right, slowly pulling his hand out from her sweater.

My mouth fell open as I stumbled backward at the sight. He slid a gun out of her sweater and into his backpack.

"The gun," I thought. That was where the gun came from. But why? Ashley wasn't the type to have a weapon, either. She was from a good home. True, it was only her and her father since her mom passed, but still. None of this made any sense.

"Why did she have a gun," I thought.

As Dre zipped his bag close, she erupted.

"He ruined me! Do you not understand?" Ashley knelt as her back pressed against the brick wall, crying into her hands. "I'm not me anymore. I tried so hard." Her tears seeped through her fingers.

"I tried so hard to go back to the way things were. I can't." She pulled the cuff of her sweater down and wiped her nose. "I just can't. I don't want to be here anymore."

"It'll be okay; let me help you," Dre pleaded. He knelt beside her, rubbing her shoulders. She jumped at the contact. My heart broke with every whimper that escaped her lips.

"You can't help me; no one can."

"Ash!" Dre's voice cracked and his eyes began to weld. She sat there rocking back and forth, silent as time seemed to stand still.

Ashley stood up and he did the same. She placed her hand on his chest, staring into his chocolate eyes. Dre stared at her hand as if it held all the answers.

She exhaled deeply and said, "I'm sorry. I'm fine, Dre." Her head nodded back and forth. "I'm just tired. I just need to sleep. I'm going home to sleep."

"Ash, I'll go with you. Let me go with you." Dre reached for her hand, but she pulled away.

"No!" she shouted. Her hand waved in the air as if she had realized her tone. "No," she said calmly. "I want to be alone. Please, let me be alone. You can't fix me." She placed her palm against his cheek. "I know you want to, but you just can't."

She leaned in and hugged him, resting her head on his chest. Dre wrapped his arms around her. When his hands found her back, she jumped slightly but didn't pull away.

She tilted her head and whispered, "I'm sorry. You deserve better." Then she stepped back.

My heart shattered once again. She bit the corner of her lower lip as she stared into his eyes. This wasn't the same Ashley I knew. Her confident swagger had dissipated and her thirst for life vanished. She had changed. He had changed her.

As she walked away, Dre reached out for her hand.

"Then, promise me one thing," he said.

She turned her head, not entirely looking back.

"Promise we can talk tomorrow."

She paused and looked down.

"Promise," he demanded.

She faced away from him.

"Promise," she whispered.

His hand slowly unwrapped around hers as I watched her walk away. My heart broke with every step she took. I turned away and pressed my back against the wall.

I didn't understand what was going on. Why did Ashley have a gun and why didn't Dre just turn it in? Most importantly, I wanted to know why the person I entrusted with all my secrets kept this one from me.

My body went limp and I collapsed into death-like darkness. As my soul plummeted into the abyss, my mind froze with questions. And then, the light returned.

CHAPTER 13

MY EYES SHOT OPEN as the present came alive again. I let out an audible gasp as my body jerked forward. I was back in class and the world remained just as I left it.

"Are you okay?" Her voice was soft to ensure she didn't disturb the class.

Forcing myself to take slow, deliberate breaths, I turned and looked at Kim. I stiffened, clenching my jaw as my teeth ground down to nubs. My neck ached.

"Breathe, it's okay," she said barely above a whisper.

"I'm fine!" I whispered, but even my whisper was abrasive.

"It's just that," she stuttered. Her finger pointed towards my face. "It's your nose."

My eyebrows rose as my hand checked my nose. It was wet. I looked down to find drips of blood pooling at my desk. Pinching my nose, I raised my other hand but was cut off by the school bell.

"Are you okay? Here's a Kleenex." Kim stretched her hand with a small white cloth dangling from her fingertips.

I stared. I didn't want to accept it, but my nose was a bloody mess. I yanked the Kleenex out of her hand.

"Thanks," I said flatly.

"No problem. If you want, I can —"

"No, thank you."

I stood up and followed the rest of the class out the door. When I stepped out, I looked back and my body jerked to the side. I inadvertently ran into another student.

"Oh, sorry, I was …," I began, turning towards the student.

His eyes narrowed and his lips flattened. Erik's head tilted to the side as his eyes burrowed through me. His dead eyes forced anger to pool inside of me instantly.

"Watch it. You almost got blood on me." The disgust in his eyes was gut-wrenching. I wanted to swing so badly but now wasn't the time.

I had gotten used to the looks of pity from other students. There is nothing like being the sister of the boy who was killed and the best friend of the most disloyal person in history. So, I decided not to also be known as the girl whose nose bled all over a racist little prick.

Erik snickered and peered into the classroom. His eyes honed in on Kim as she shuffled to the door. He turned back to me, smiling. I sharpened my eyes and headed to get cleaned up. This was going to be a long week.

CHAPTER 14

AUTUMN FOUND ME IN the bathroom. Her arms wrapped around me while I finished dabbing my wet face with paper towels.

"Hey, girlie. You, okay?" Autumn asked while checking herself out in the mirror. Her thumb massaged her extended lashes, which danced with every blink. With puckered lips, she then slid her lip gloss on, which brightened her already gorgeous lips.

"Yeah, just a nosebleed," I said.

"What happened?"

"No clue just started in class. I'm alright, though. Thanks for checking in on me," I said. I shot her a smile through her reflection.

"You know I got you, girl!" Her body flipped around and she leaned against the counter. "So, I have a favor to ask."

"Okay, what's up?" I threw the last of my paper towels in the overflowing trash.

"I think," she said slowly, "you should come on my podcast and talk about —"

"Absolutely not. I'm not —," I started.

"Not what? A person who has been through a lot? A person who lost someone close to them and needs to find a way to heal? You're exactly the person who needs to be in front of a crowd."

I shook my head.

"Miracle, the news is slandering his name. We need to —"

"No, Autumn." My voice was so commanding that it surprised her. Heck, it surprised me too. She stared at me and I did the same to her.

"No," I repeated.

She nodded her head and waved her hands in the air.

"Okay. Okay. But if you ever change your mind —" she said.

"I know where to find you." I shot her a half-smile, grabbed my stuff, and headed out.

CHAPTER 15

THE REST OF THE day was uneventful. There were a few more movies in class and some more daydreaming about Dre and Ashley. I went around the school during breaks, looking for Ashley, but it seemed like she was a ghost. No one had seen or heard from her in a while.

As the last bell rang, I proceeded to the school bus and nearly fainted at the sight. My fist clenched as I watched Erik standing in the corner next to the bike rack. Kim was with him.

They didn't see me, but I definitely saw them. Erik brushed his hand against her arm. It was very sensual, especially considering the monster doing the act.

Kim stood there, motionless. I couldn't see her face since her back was to me. But still, my stomach curled. My tongue poked against my cheek as I exhaled deeply. Another knife had been plunged into my back.

"Oh, Kim," I whispered.

I shook my head and then headed on the bus. Moments later, Kim slithered on. Her lips curled as her usually pale face was colored with a red hue—no doubt from embarrassment.

She made her way to the back, occasionally pausing to wait for the slower students to cram in their seats. When she saw me, her hand flew to her lips. Her eyes bulged. I shot my head down, pretending not to notice. I never thought she would betray me…twice.

My sweater hoody flung over my face and I slid my earbuds in. My head rested on the cold seat as NF's voice drowned the background noise.

"How could you leave us so unexpected?
We waited, we waited,
For you but you just left us,
We needed you. I needed you."

My face softened while his words hit my soul differently than before. This song was fitting, too fitting. I closed my eyes and let the music take over. As it did, so did the darkness. I plunged forward as my limbs waved in the air. NF slowly faded to nothing and only the darkness again existed.

CHAPTER 16

*"I'D PRAY FOR YOU more than me,
I'd cross the oceans and swim the seas."*

A teasing voice blasted through the darkness. I recognized the song from the pier, but the words had lost their meaning. Even the tone transformed. There was no rhythm, pacing, or emotion, yet, every word cut like a knife.

The screams of a female followed the taunts. My eyes quickly flashed open. I stood behind a run-down shack. Its weathered brown wood splinted at the edges. Blood spray-painted the walls of the building.

"You want to touch my girl?" someone screamed.

I sprinted to the corner of the shack and watched. A teen stood in a field of knee-high grass. A vast meadow lay behind him as the ocean-colored sky hung in the background.

His hand flew through the air. Upon impact, a gush of crimson flew through the air, landing on the nearby daisies.

"Stop it right now, Tyler."

Two other guys were holding back a young woman. Her arms stretched out as she struggled to get free. It was the girl from the photo. Suzanne. No, Susan.

"Let go of me," she growled.

"Is this what you want?" Tyler turned to her. As his frame narrowed, I could see the target of his rage. Billy (the young man I met on a pier singing sweet lullabies to his true love) sat on his knees with his arms extended, held up by another two guys. His previous kind-hearted soul was replaced by that of a battered animal, caged for being himself.

"You want him over me? Huh?" His voice was cold with anger. Another punch slashed across Billy's face. His head jerked back, then hung in pain. The blood pooled at his feet. Signs of a black eye were already evident.

"I swear, Tyler. As God is my witness, if you touch him again, I will kill you myself."

Tyler turned. Fire roared in his wide eyes. His left hand cupped the young man's head as another fist plunged into his dark skin.

"Tyler!" she shouted, her southern drawl coming out.

He wrapped his fingers around Billy's neck. Large veins pulsated throughout Tyler's hands as Billy gasped. His eyes bulged as the simple task of breathing became impossible.

"And if ya ever touch my girl again, yous dead. Ya, hear me? Dead!" He coughed up a giant wad of spit, which soon dribbled down Billy's face.

Tyler nodded at the two guys holding the man at bay. As they released him, Billy collapsed to the ground, coughing in pain. Blood shot out of his mouth, blending in with the already-soaked earth.

Susan got to her feet. Her eyes locked on Billy quivering in the dirt. Tyler and his crew strode past her. A mischievous smile crossed his face while staring brazenly into her eyes. His posture, sinister smile, and demeanor were a twin to Erik. I guess evil existed everywhere.

Susan's steps were slow. Her feet delicately pressed against the ground while she advanced. She stood over Billy's trembling body. Her tears poured; her face melted.

She knelt and hovered her hand over his body, scared any contact would cause even more pain to him. She lowered her head and whispered into his ear. I was too far to hear, but she stood up and walked away after she was done.

My heart sank at the sight of him. When I first met him, he was filled with happiness and unparalleled love and now I see why. His passion was unobtainable because of the world he lived in. His life would be so different if he were born thirty years later.

I took a step forward and stopped mid-stride. Off in the distance, a figure appeared. I couldn't determine who it was, but they honed in on me. Their darting gaze read awareness, awareness that I didn't belong. My stomach churned as our minds engaged in a distant telepathic war.

Their head lowered and they barrelled forward. The mysterious being took shape. Her strides were extended. Her arms cut through the air. My mouth fell open as I shuffled backward.

"What the hell," I mumbled.

Her run quickened as she passed Billy, not giving him a second thought. My thoughts became fuzzy and I didn't know what to do. Her silver eyes pierced through me.

"What the hell," I repeated

Without another thought, I did what I did best; I ran. I turned away and zipped around the building. My feet kicked up the dirt as my legs pressed my body forward. As I passed another worn-down shack, I turned around and those grey predator eyes were still locked on me.

When I turned back, my body collapsed into an empty void of life and the world went dark again. The calm silence was welcoming.

I jerked forward, hitting the chair in front of me. The girl in front of me turned around.

"What the hell?"

She stared as my chest heaved up and down.

"Hey, are you okay?" she asked, switching her tone.

I nodded and lowered my head.

"Sorry," I mumbled.

She turned back around as I blew out several harsh breaths.

"What the heck was that? Who the hell was she," I thought.

When my breathing slowed, I slowly raised my head, rotating my already tensed shoulders. My head turned to the left, peering out the window. Then, back to the right where Kim stared at me.

Her eyebrows rose and she shot me a curious look. My head snapped back down and I stayed that way the entire way back home.

CHAPTER 17

THE SLURPEE SPLASHED AGAINST my taste buds, bringing a smile to my lips. Greg sat next to me on the curb of the convenience store. Our shoulders kissed as the rest of the world zoomed by.

"So, what did she say?"

"Nothing. I mean, she didn't even see me," I said.

"What are you going to do about it?"

"Nothing. She made her bed. That's on her." I stared forward, not looking at anything in particular. I was too young to deal with all this drama. I mean, life wasn't supposed to be hard until after high school, right?

"Yeah, I guess," he said. "You know, I spoke to her a few times since the trial."

My eyes shot up and my head swiveled to meet his.

"What the hell, Greg."

"She called me," he shrugged.

"Oh, and that makes it better? You know what, you do you."

"Miracle, it's not like—," he said, but before he could finish, I was already on my feet, storming away.

"Miracle, wait." He raced to me, grabbing my hand to slow me down. I couldn't take any more of this heartbreak.

"Would you stop! Miracle?" He extended his arm again and his hands found my wrist. He stopped me with a gentle tug and managed to wrap his other hand around my waist. Then our eyes met and he mouthed the word stop.

I stood there. My eyes shot daggers through his, but his only counterattack was that of a soft, gentle smile.

"It's not even like that. You know I have your back. I'm team Miracle all the way. I even made t-shirts." His voice was as gentle as his soul.

I pursed my lips for a second. Then, I shot him a slight smile as my breathing slowed. My shoulders slumped and I let out an audible sigh.

"Okay," I finally said.

"She called me because you wouldn't call her back. She just needed someone to talk to. This wasn't easy for her, Miracle."

"It wasn't easy for her? FOR HER?" My voice cracked. I shook my head as my eyes narrowed. "You know what, whatever."

Before I could storm out, he held my hand, not allowing me to leave.

"Greg, let me go," I demanded.

"Are you okay?"

"Why do you always ask me that? I'm fine," I said. My tone was something Greg wasn't used to, at least not from me. But I was tired of his constant worry. I didn't need a parent. I needed a friend or boyfriend or whatever he was. That was what I needed.

Maybe it wasn't just about Kim. My mind was still clouded with thoughts of Dre with Ashley. And who the heck was that mysterious girl chasing me? I might have been a little more defensive than usual. Greg didn't deserve my verbal attack, but he repeatedly asked me the same question.

He gently wrapped his hands around my wrists, but I yanked them away.

"I don't want to hold hands. I want to know why you keep asking me if I'm ok." I began. "Ever since the trial, you've been—"

He gripped my wrists again and raised them to eye level.

"Look," he demanded.

My head tilted to the side and I frowned. Then, my face softened. My hands were shaking. It was subtle, but only those who really paid attention would notice them.

I broke my hands away and stared at them.

"This isn't right. I'm just…I mean, I'm just tired." I racked my brain for a viable excuse. But my words lacked the confidence needed to convince Greg or myself.

"They've been shaking since Dre died," he said, barely above a whisper.

I looked up and met his eyes. There was no pity in them, just concern.

"Soooo, about Kim," he said. My head lowered once again. "I think she needs you."

I took a breath and allowed him to continue.

"It was nearly impossible for her to confront you about Dre. She didn't want to believe what she saw. But she saw," he said hesitating, "what she saw."

"So, she saw Dre aim the gun at the officers? Really, Greg?"

"Yeah." He paused. "That was her perspective. We both know she was wrong, but that's what she thought." He waited to see if his words had any effect on me. They didn't.

"Anyways, things got worse for her after the trial too."

"Oh, did her brother die?" I asked sarcastically.

He paused for a second and then responded.

"Yes."

I looked into his eyes and realized he was right. My head turned away. My eyes began to water as my hand quickly wiped away the tears.

"What am I supposed to do? Huh? I can't talk to her. I don't want to see her. I'm just not ready yet. Okay?" I turned to walk away, but he grabbed my hand, pulling me back.

"I'm not asking you to forgive her. Just think about what she's going through."

I turned back to face him. My sweet Greg. Always defending others even when they didn't deserve it. It reminded me of Dre.

I stepped closer to him and pressed my lips to his. My tears soaked his cheeks as my eyes shut and I savored the moment. Yeah, I cherished the thought of him as my boyfriend.

CHAPTER 18

WHEN OUR LIPS FINALLY separated, I stared into his eyes and smiled.

"You're amazing. You know that?" I asked, pressing my head to his chest.

"Actually, I did. I'm kind of a big deal around here," he said.

I pushed his chest away.

"Okay, Mr. Big Deal." We shared a mutual laugh.

When our hands interlocked again, I noticed the driver of a blue car watching us. When he saw me notice him, his head turned away.

"Come on," I said.

"What's wrong?"

"It's another reporter. This is like the 7th reporter that's been following me. They just want a scoop about my brother. It's getting old. Come on."

I turned to the vehicle, dragging Greg along with me.

"Woah. This isn't a good idea. Don't you watch scary movies?"

"Boy, come on," I said. But before we could reach the car, the driver stepped out. I felt Greg tug on my arm, forcing me backward.

"Greg, stop. It's just another reporter, I'll—"

"That's not a reporter."

I stopped mid-stride, forcing Greg to slam into me.

"You know him?" I asked.

"I recognize him from the TV. You know him too."

I turned back to face the man, who was roughly 20 yards away. He was a middle-aged man with a scar over his right eyebrow. Nothing too remarkable. But his deep-set eyes reminded me of … oh my God. It was him.

"What do you want?" I yelled. Greg pulled me back and stood in front of me, with one hand extended and the other wrapped around me.

The man lifted his hands in a defensive posture, showing he meant no harm. He had no weapons.

"I just wanted to talk," he said, shooting us a pained stare.

"Sir, we don't want any trouble," Greg said as we slowly backed away. "And we didn't do anything wrong."

Noticing our fear, the man slowly stopped his approach.

"I'm not here to cause any trouble. I just wanted to say …," he paused, staring at the sidewalk. "I'm sorry about your brother. I truly am."

We both stared at him. A grimace set on his lips as he shifted about, lowering his gaze.

"You're sorry? You're sorry," I repeated, leaning my body forward. "You're the reason why he's dead." My finger aimed straight at him.

He let out an audible sigh and his shoulders slumped. He shook his head, not in denial but in disgust.

"It wasn't supposed to go down like that. Once that first shot rang out, I…I thought your brother shot first. I didn't know. My job is all about split-second decisions I didn't…." His lips clenched together like a mysterious being silenced his thoughts; his eyes gained a maroon hue.

Greg turned to me and I shrugged.

"I'm sorry. I'm sorry about Andre."

"Don't you dare say his name!" I lunged forward, pounding the officer's chest with my hands. He just stood there, taking it, tears in his eyes. Finally, Greg snatched me back.

The pain I felt when he spoke Dre's name was like being back on those stairs watching his motionless body, watching every bullet rip through his flesh as the blood pooled at his feet.

My hand flew to my chest as the pain became unbearable. The tears flowed as I dropped down to my knees.

"Don't say his name," I mumbled, barely audible through the tears. Greg and the man just stood there, not knowing how to react. Greg turned to the man.

"You should go, Sir."

The officer nodded. He reached into his shirt pocket, pulled out a small rectangular card, and handed it to Greg. Then, he turned back to his car.

Greg stood over me, protecting me while the car drove past us. He knelt with me and pulled me into his arms.

CHAPTER 19

"HEY, MADEA," I SAID while walking through the door.

"Hey, baby. Have you seen these Kordasians? I like that Kim girl." She bobbed her head in enjoyment, pointing to the television scene.

"It's Kardashians. Yeah, Kim is cool." I turned to make my way to my room, but she stopped me.

"Come here. Sit down with me for a second." She patted the sofa cushion next to her. Her eyes followed me as I walked.

"So, Bubble Gum, I heard about that girl you used to hang out with and what she did," Madea said, drawing her eyebrows together.

Why the hell is everyone talking about Kim, I thought.

She turned to me. "You, okay?"

I rubbed my wrists but didn't look up.

"I'm fine, Madea. Promise." I threw her a slight smile, which her grandmotherly instincts quickly rejected.

"Tell me about her," she said.

"Who? Kim?"

She nodded.

"She's Kim. She's the one who said Dre—"

"No, Bubble Gum. I know what she did. Tell me about who she is. As a person." She leaned back, stacked her hands on the bible resting on her lap, and gave me the floor.

I studied her for a second. She was serious.

"Well," I started, closing my eyes, "She is, uh, I don't know. She's smart," I stammered. "Very smart. Like reads-for-fun type of smart." I paused. My face dropped. "She's sweet."

"How so?" she asked.

"I don't know." I shook my head and shrugged. "Like once I had a bad day and she bought me this little toy. It was like a pink unicorn or something. I don't know. But she bought it with her own money. We were like ten or something." I fidgeted with my fingers. "She was saving to buy some science lab thing but decided to use the money to cheer me up."

"I'd call that sweet." Her eyes laid steady on mine as if she understood. "What else?"

"I don't know," I shrugged.

"Is she honest?" she asked.

"Yes, Ma'am."

Her lips parted as if she was about to speak and then they closed as she looked down at the worn black book. A soft sigh emerged from her lips.

"For every dark night, there's a brighter day," she said.

"Ephesians 4:32," I said. I hoped my confident tone would fool her into believing I actually read the bible every day like she once demanded I do.

"No. Tupac."

"Madea!" My head shot up with wide eyes.

A playful, sweet smile spread across her face, highlighting her wrinkles.

"Just because I carry a bible don't mean Madea ain't street," she said. Her shoulders bounced up and down with her laughter.

"Madea!" I repeated. Her laughter was contagious.

"The point is, child, that sometimes we must forgive one dark night and focus on the bright days. Does that make sense, baby girl?"

I nodded. She cupped my chin and lifted my head to meet her eyes.

"Forgiveness is stronger than any hate we feel in our hearts. Don't let this hate consume you. Don't let it end a beautiful relationship."

I didn't have the heart to tell her my love for Kim was well past gone. Instead, I stared into her gray eyes and saw truth. This truth had survived hatred, bigotry, racism, and the death of a spouse. This truth was real.

"Yes, ma'am," I mumbled.

CHAPTER 20

"ALRIGHT, LADIES. HERE'S $30 for some pizza," my dad said, reaching out with a handful of cash.

The aroma of his cologne subtly floated in the room.

"Uh, Dad, why are you all dressed up? You don't need a collared shirt to go bowling."

"Actually, you do," he joked. "But I," he said, doing a little twirl, "have a date. How do I look?" His chest thrust out as he flaunted a knowing smile.

Madea didn't speak. Instead, she turned to me and watched my reaction while I picked my jaw off the floor.

"But, dad, what about mom? I mean, you're only separated, right? I thought you decided not to finalize the divorce." My words trailed off. My eyes zoomed from dad to Madea and back.

He reached his hand to me, but I jerked away, leaned back on the couch, and crossed my arms. Maybe I was acting a little immature, but this was my dad. He loved my mom and I knew it.

He would beam whenever her name was brought up, like a little schoolgirl having their first crush. Heck, he still mooned over her, calling her to see if she wanted anything from Starbucks even though she didn't live with us anymore. He still loved her. He had to. I didn't want them to end up like Greg's parents.

Dad slowly approached but was cut off by the doorbell. His shoulders dropped and he lowered his head.

"I can't wait for her forever, Bubble Gum. I will always love her, but," he paused. He grimaced as if in pain. He sighed and walked to the door.

Madea squeezed my hand. Could she see the pain in my eyes? My heartbreak?

"Hey, I know this is strange," my dad said, standing at the open door, "but I'd like you to meet my daughter. She means the world to me and I'd never want to break her heart." The last part he nearly screamed. "Do you mind?"

My heart swelled as thoughts of my mom floated into my mind: her smile when she looked into his eyes and the flirty way she'd always find ways to touch him, even if it was a simple tap on his hand - her favorite was the butt slaps, which drove me crazy, especially in public.

I didn't turn to look. Instead, my eyes rummaged around the kitchen. The sense of being watched rushed over me. His new "girlfriend" must be surveying me with her eyes.

Wonder where he met her? Work? Gym? Wait, did my dad have an online dating account? A bit of vomit got caught in my throat at the thought.

"Miracle?" my dad said.

My head slowly turned, searching for this beast of a woman who dared take my dad away. Her spiked hair was black, sprinkled with a grey zest. Her piercing stare made my heartbeat skip as her chubby cheeks framed her thick dark red lips. She smiled and that was all I needed.

I ran into my mom's arms, squeezing tightly. I felt the warmth of her breath on my neck as she pressed her head against mine. Her heartbeat roared with excitement.

"Hey, Bubble Gum." Her voice was just as magical as I remembered.

I pulled myself away from her, wiping my tears.

"What are you doing here?"

"Someone asked me on a date." She nodded in my dad's direction. He, of course, stood there with a guilty smile across his face.

"He made me think you were some girl he met online who hated kids and anyone named Miracle," I said.

"Hey, I didn't say all that now."

"He sho did," Madea chimed in.

"Momma," my dad exclaimed.

I pressed myself into my mom once more. She smelled of lavender.

"Does this mean you're coming back?" I asked.

"We're going to take this slow, sweety. I still have a few things to fix before moving back. But I'm doing a lot better lately," she said, nodding joyfully.

"Therapy is doing wonders," my dad said.

"Therapy?"

"Actually, it's group therapy for parents who lost a child," she said.

"Do Black people go to therapy?" I asked, wrinkling my nose.

"Yes," my dad replied. "There's even another Black person in our group."

I turned back to her. "Our group? Wait, you go together?" My eyes ping pong between my parents

"Uh, Clyde, we're the only Black people at those meetings," my mom said.

"Nah, what about that one guy, Marcus? He's always there. He's actually my favorite person to talk to there, besides you, of course," my dad said.

"Babes, that's the janitor. He comes in early for the doughnuts. You never noticed the broom?"

We all stared at my dad.

"I just assumed he hated dirt. Dang, I gave him my phone number in case he ever needed to talk." Dad's shoulders slumped while the rest of us laughed at his confusion.

CHAPTER 21

AFTER SEVERAL SLICES OF Hawaiian pizza – and yes, I put pineapples on my pizza – I took advantage of my dad being on his hot date and headed out the door. Madea was already curled up on the couch watching a marathon of "Kordasians," as she put it.

When I arrived at the convenience store, Greg leaned against the building, his fingers furiously typing away on his phone.

"Thanks for meeting me," I said. "And I'm sorry about earlier."

"Don't worry about it. I get it," Greg said. He smiled sweetly, leaning down and pressing his thick lips against mine. His mom was off tonight, so he wasn't stuck watching his two brothers for once and I was grateful.

"Man, those lips got me every time," I thought. But his sweetness had to wait. We were on a mission.

"I took your advice too," he said. "I called my dad and told him I'd meet him first before he saw the boys."

I frowned and tilted my head. I didn't remember giving him any advice, but I never turned down a compliment.

"You're welcome. It was the least I could do." My hand wrapped around the back of his neck and I lowered him in for another kiss.

"Anyways, why do you think Ashley gave Dre the gun?" Greg asked.

I wanted to tell him everything, but how could I explain this? "Oh, I can time travel and visit my relatives, so I saw Dre take the gun from Ashley and blah. Still want to date the crazy time-traveling girl with emotional issues?" He'd think I was crazy.

"Woman's intuition," I said.

He paused, wrinkling his nose.

"Mmmhmmm."

"What? It's a real thing."

"And you think Rieko knows where Ashley is?"

"Hopefully. I don't know where else to turn," I said. "I looked around at school, but she was a ghost."

We turned and walked away. Plus, it was already late on a school night, so we had to do this quickly.

My pace was nearly a run as we jetted down Sierra Highway. The darkness of the night provided an even somber appearance to the vast desert town. The red and orange lights of the cars blinked as cars sprinted along the streets.

Using red lights to catch his breath, I was sure Greg regretted agreeing to tag along. He was lucky I didn't run, which every nerve in my body wanted to do.

We stared as a group of supped-up Honda Civics hovered inches from the ground. Their spoilers sliced through the air as their speakers rattled their trunks. Some sounded pretty good, with bass that could rattle your bones, while most of them just seemed like the speakers were too much for the tiny cars.

We zipped past the auto dealership, but my pace slowed a bit when the enticing aroma of the Mexican restaurant waffled in the air.

"No. Focus," I told myself.

As we approached the apartment complex, an invisible force stopped me in my tracks. My breaths poured out in short bursts. My insides turned with every breath. My fingers caressed my forearm, trying to soothe my nerves.

"What's going on?" Greg asked, panting. His hands fell to his knees, trying to recover his breath.

I twisted my head, glaring around the light blue apartments, not really seeing anything. I didn't know what I was looking for. My feet were frozen to the ground and my heart slammed against my chest, tightening with every beat.

"I can't do this." I turned to walk away.

"Wait, what the…What's going on?" He reached out and grabbed my hand.

My eyes swelled as a deep burning sensation pierced through my chest. My breathing became labored as an acid-like taste swam in my throat. My hands flung to my knees. My dinner reappeared.

"Miracle." Greg's voice was soft.

As I wrenched over, I felt a gentle tug on my hair. Greg clung to my braids so they wouldn't get soiled.

After several minutes, I finally stood up and turned to walk home, head held down. Greg turned back to the complex and then quickly joined me.

"I'm sorry, I didn't even think that—"

"This isn't on you, Greg. This was my call. I can't go back there. I haven't been back since —."

Greg swooped me in his arms, covering me like a blanket. My head pressed against his chest. The subtle drums of his heartbeat consumed me.

"I thought I could, but I can't. I just can't," I mumbled through the tears.

"Yeah, okay. I get it," he whispered.

Greg walked me back to my apartment and promised to be there the next time I decided to go back.

"Even if it takes a hundred tries, I'll be there every time," he said.

I placed my hand on his chest and gave him a half-smile. For a moment, I got lost in his eyes. He leaned in for a kiss, but I immediately stiff-armed him.

"Dude, no. I just threw up. Gross."

"Oh yeah, good point. Plus, you have a little something-something in your teeth," he said, pointing at my mouth.

"Oh my God, do I?" My hands flung to my mouth as my head twisted back.

"Nah, I'm kidding." He laughed until I swatted his arm.

He extended his arm and we returned to our old goodbye, a sweet and innocent fist bump.

CHAPTER 22

AFTER SCHOOL THE FOLLOWING day, my dad took Madea to In and Out since all her friends were raving about it. This meant there was no rush for me to get home after school. So, I took a detour.

The park was the perfect spot to get away. Many people were scattered throughout the large park, but that wasn't unusual. The benches under the pavilion were empty, minus two older men playing chess. I sat on the furthest bench from them and enjoyed the view.

Yellow leaves floated to the ground as squirrels raced around, looking for their next meal. The alluring aroma of orange poppies enticed my nose while the wind gently kissed the flowers waving to the world. It was peaceful here. It was perfect.

My parents always brought Dre and me here for all his baseball games. But my favorite was the annual poppy festival. There would be so much food; funnel cakes, giant pickles with peppermints buried inside, and cotton candy. It was one of the few days I looked forward to every year.

My finger pressed against my phone as my playlist appeared. I scrolled through, trying to find something relaxing. I tapped Willow Marie's song, *Blessed*, and folded my arms over the table. My head rested against my forearms as I watched two toddlers clap their hands in an attempt to catch bubbles floating in the air.

When the music began, my eyes closed out the world and all that remained was Willow Marie's angelic voice.

> *"You are what I need*
> *You're my everything*
> *I feel blessed (blessed),*
> *I feel blessed (blessed)...."*

The familiar cold chill sprung up against my arms. My chest expanded as the cool air rushed into my lungs. Then, it happened. My soul plunged into the abyss. I was getting used to the rush of falling.

CHAPTER 23

HUMMING SLOWLY CREPT INTO the darkness, filling the silence. When I opened my eyes, the world came alive again and the familiar smell of roses hit my nose first, followed by the unmistakable scent of freshly cooked food.

My eyes scanned the room as I sat at a large wooden table. Giant plates of food were displayed in front of me, enticing my every taste bud. Piles of cornbread with butter oozing down the side and a platter of fried chicken yearned to be tasted. Sweet melons teased my eyes as they lay perfectly on each other in their bowl. My mouth watered at the sight.

The room was just as fancy as the spread. Large picture frames hung on the walls, highlighting beautifully dressed men and women. Under the food dishes sat a large white tablecloth, which held perfectly folded napkins shaped like flowers.

Three young light-skinned women approached the table and began serving food to those seated. An older Black woman stood in the corner as if she was supervising the others. One of the younger women stood next to the table and shoveled a pile of mashed potatoes onto a plate.

I nearly jumped out of my seat as I recognized the older man sitting at the head of the table. Before, he had hollered at two slaves dancing for a piece of cake. Now, his head was filled with wrinkles and dark spots, but his long white beard flowed the same. His eyes drooped more, but it was definitely him.

Alongside him was a modest-looking woman, nothing too special about her. She busied herself, inspecting the spoon. The older woman in the corner lifted her chin, observing the woman's facial expression.

"Ma'am, yous need another spoon? I can have Marybelle fetch ya one," the older woman said. She pointed her finger at one of the girls and motioned to the kitchen.

"Darling, I don't think these new ones are going to work out. This silverware is simply dreadful," the woman said. "Heavens to Betsy, just look at these spots!"

"Momma, those spots have been on our silverware for years. It ain't they fault."

"Hush up now, Eliza," the woman commanded.

Eliza, I thought. It was her. Her head had narrowed, her baby cheeks had vanished, but the hair…those eyes…her smile. It was the little girl too. My head spun in a million circles.

"Randal, you okay? You look a little off," the man said.

"I hope it's not that flu that's been going 'round here. Half the slaves are sleeping the day away in their beds."

"Cots, Momma. They don't have beds," Eliza said.

"You know what I mean. Don't correct me, child."

"Randal?"

My attention returned to the man as the realization he was talking to me finally clicked. Then, everyone stared at me.

"Willie-Mae, would you please," the woman commanded, gesturing towards me.

The older woman nodded and made her way next to me. I stared as she raised her worn hand and placed the back of it against my forehead. Her hands felt soft and warm. She reminded me of Madea.

"No feva, Ma'am." She turned to the woman. "Yous want me to run a bath for him?"

"No, I'm fine, but thank you," I said.

Heads tilted as the wandering eyes grew wide.

"You sure you okay, Randal? You seem awfully polite right now. No offense, son, but that's not in your nature," the man said.

"I'm fine."

"Just look at these spots." All attention went back to the woman as she inspected another spoon. "That's probably where he got the sickness," she said.

The kitchen door opened as another young woman walked in. Her skin didn't hold the same lightness as the others. Instead, her skin reflected the smooth brownness of a Hershey's kiss. Her eyes filled with dark pools of fear.

"Massa', yous wanted to see Lizzie?"

"Awh, yes. I sho' did." The older man turned his head. The mere act seemed like it caused him a great deal of pain. I drew my eyebrows together as he spoke.

"Get to where I can see you, child." She did as she was told.

He then turned to Willie-Mae and nodded. She walked over to an old white China set, where a black book lay on top. She grabbed it and placed it in front of Lizzie.

Lizzie's eyes widened as her eyebrows shot up. Fear rang through my chest as I imagined all the cruelty that would happen to this young girl.

CHAPTER 24

THE MAN PLACED HIS hand on his cane, perched alongside his chair. He fidgeted with the round knob that sat on top of the cane. Every breath he took was labored and sweat streamed down his flushed face.

"Go ahead, Lizzie." His eyes honed on her. The room went silent. What kind of torture did he have in mind for this young girl? She couldn't have been more than 13.

"Yes, Massa," she said. Her voice was soft but shaky. Her skinny fingers wrapped around the cover and she opened the book. Pages flipped open, making a propeller-like noise. Her finger roamed through the pages and then she looked up.

"Go ahead." A dry cough escaped his lips, which he quickly covered with a white handkerchief from his vest pocket.

She began. "Let the wi…wic..wicked…." She looked up again and the man nodded. So, she continued, "forsake their ways." Her words were slow and concentrated. A simple sentence took minutes to read, but she kept going, finally ending with "and the unrighteous their thoughts."

"That's better, Lizzie. Keep practicing," Eliza smiled.

"Sho is." A gentle smile crossed the man's face. The woman, not so much.

"What is the point of teaching them to read? All they need to learn to do is cook, clean, and provide me with a spotless spoon. They can't even do that right."

A soft groan emerged from Eliza's lips.

"Do you have something to say, Eliza? If not, watch yourself, or I'll have you living out there with those animals. Ya want that, huh?"

"No, Ma'am," Eliza said. A hint of disrespect still lingered in her tone.

"I have had it with you." The woman jumped up and slammed her napkin onto the table.

"Darling, take a breath. You gettin' carried away, and you know …" A bout of hoarse coughs sent the man's body flinging forward. Eliza leaned towards him, as did Willie-May.

"Massa', you, okay?" Willie-May asked.

"Of course, he's not okay. He's having a coughing fit because of you and you," the woman pointed to Eliza. "Lord help him, he don't die because of y'all."

I stared at the older man. The first time I saw him, he was smiling and laughing. Living like time was plentiful, but this version of him was shriveled and weak. Even his voice was more subdued.

With his handkerchief covering his mouth, the last of the coughs subsided. A trail of saliva hung between his lips and the cloth fabric.

"Y'all both be the death of me," he mumbled.

The woman knitted her eyes and a wave of red splashed across her face.

"Me? Oh, no, this is all you. It's your fault this little girl thinks she's a princess. It's your fault these slaves think they free. It's—," her rant was interrupted by the glaring eyes of the old man.

Her body softened, yet there was still anger in her soul. She let out an audible sigh.

"Please excuse me. I seemed to have lost my appetite." She slowly backed her chair up and proceeded to walk out. The man reached for her arm, but she quickly batted it away and stormed out of the room.

The rest of the group carried on. Eliza and the man proceeded to eat as if this was normal. The young women retreated into the kitchen as Willie-May took a seat on a wooden stool in the corner of the room. Her feet dangled from the floor. She reminded me of a child placed in time-out.

"Excuse me, Massa?" Willie-May's voice rang out.

"What is it, Willie-May?" the elderly man said, his mouth filled with a mix between mashed potatoes and corn.

"We's 'ppreciate yous teaching us how to read. That's mighty kind of ya, Massa'."

I stared at Willie-May, trying to see if she was joking. "Teaching us how to read." The words were English, but the meaning was foreign to me.

The older man stopped chewing. His hand inches from his lips, dangling the drumstick in the air. Then, his eyes went to Willie-May and then to Eliza. Eliza peeked up with a mischievous grin.

"Thank Ms. Eliza, Willie-May. Let's just say she opened my eyes." Eliza's white teeth shined against the chandelier's light above the table. She slid her hand towards him and he did the same.

"Well, thank ya, Ms. Eliza. We sho do…" The older man coughed viciously before she could finish. His body jerked forward as his face convulsed in a grimace. His hand clenched his chest as the white fabric returned to his lips.

Eliza jumped up and ran to him. Willie-May did the same. The coughing continued almost rhythmically. I slid back, scraping the chair legs against the hardwood floor.

I reached out my hand and my soul collapsed into a void of darkness. The weightless feeling encased my body as my mind went blank.

CHAPTER 25

I'VE NEVER THOUGHT I would question my sanity, but lately, all I did was question it. These "episodes" were becoming more frequent. Thankfully, my stalker hadn't shown her face recently.

Unfortunately, there was no one I could turn to, and no resources to go to. Heck, even Google would probably end with disappointing results. It was useless. I gathered my things and left the park.

The sunset sky was painted a beautiful orange and yellow. It made my walk home even more enjoyable. As I crossed West Avenue K, the familiar feeling of being watched took over me.

I panned to the right and left, but nothing. Then I looked behind me and noticed a black car slowly creeping up. When I stopped, so did it. My first thought was it was the police officer again, tailing me.

I didn't have enough energy to run and evade the car, so I did the one thing Greg would hate.

Tap tap tap.

The passenger-side window lowered and a grease cloud floated to the sky. I peered inside, finding five or so hamburger wrappers littered in the stained backseat.

The driver was a short man with squared glasses pressed against his face. Stubble covered his cheeks as if he hadn't shaved in a few days. I leaned forward.

"Why are you following me?" I asked.

"Uh…sorry, I didn't mean to freak you out," he stuttered.

My eyebrows rosed as I gripped my phone even tighter. I'd hoped he was unaware he was being recorded. It was dumb to walk up to the car, but I wasn't dumb enough not to record it.

"I'm Dale Youngblood. You can call me Dale if you'd like."

I scrunched up my face.

"Or not. I'm a reporter with FNN-7 and wondered if I could ask you a few questions."

I stood up and turned to walk away.

"Another reporter," I mumbled.

I could hear him shouting for me to come back, but his words bounced off my ears and landed in the trash, where they belonged.

CHAPTER 26

WHEN I GOT BACK home, my dad sat at the laptop. His head hovered over the keyboard as his fingers pressed each key carefully. Typing wasn't his best attribute.

I found Madea sitting on my…I mean her bed. She was studying her own assignment; the bible leaned against her lap.

I shot her a wave and then sat on my chair. My fingers spread through the pink fabric. I pushed my headphones over my ears and listened to my music while watching Madea get lost in her Bible.

Her fingers slid across the page. At times, she'd close her eyes, not to sleep but to assist her brain in soaking in the information. When her eyes reappeared, she'd take little breaks to jot down notes on her notepad, which she kept on my nightstand next to the bed.

Her fingers lifted in the air and froze there momentarily. Then, she looked at me and my body went limp as my music faded into the background. My body dove into the familiar darkness and Madea was no more.

My soul felt as if it was being pulled down. Suddenly, my body stopped falling, pressing against a wooden floor. I swayed back and forth as the sound of crashing waves lingered in the air.

CHAPTER 27

MY HEAD JERKED BACK as the stench in the air hit me first. A slight bit of vomit froze at the edge of my throat as my hand flung to my lips. My face squeezed shut as the smell burnt my nostrils.

I opened my eyes and I was surprised to find more darkness. Brief hints of light shined from openings in the walls. As the floor swayed, my body slid slightly, pressing against another figure, a woman.

Her nails dug into the ceiling as tears rolled along her face, creeping into her ears. A sense of fear roamed through my body as panic set in. I turned my head in the other direction.

Another female lay to my left. Her eyes were wide, staring into the distance. Although her body sat inches away, I feared her mind was nowhere to be found. A streak of light glistened from the cracks in the wall, revealing her half-naked body pressed against the wooden planks. That was when I realized we were on a ship.

The sounds of chains rattling came from the front of the room. A giant burst of light broke free as a large door opened, revealing the horrors held inside.

Thirty to forty women mashed inside this small room. They were squeezed inside like potatoes in a sack: no room to move, no fresh air to breathe. Arms and legs intertwined as people covered their faces from the bright light. Water leaked from the ceiling.

Suddenly, three men came slandering down the steps. Their faces wrinkled as the smell hit them, but the stench did little to wipe the smiles off their face.

"Everyone up! Head on the deck," one man screamed. His accent-rich voice boomed in the tiny room. Moans emerged from the women as they helped each other up. Their skeleton bodies inched up the steps as their backsides revealed their horrific dwellings.

I followed as the herd of malnourished souls crept forward. The sun shined high in the sky; typically, a beautiful sight. But this day, its brightness bought pain to my existence. The smell of fresh air was drowned out by the intoxicating scent of human feces and sickness. Still, the cool breeze felt good against my skin.

The men herded us into a small section in the back of this wooden mass. Our bare feet scraped against the blood-soaked deck.

As I pushed forward, I saw a giant wooden wall separating us from the men. Their condition was no better and, in some cases, even worse. Ligature marks tattooed their bare chests as their eyes searched for their lost love.

"Kopombano," a woman shouted in the crowd; men and women turned on their captives. I was thrown back as a woman lunged at the man in front of me.

He quickly retaliated as three more women jumped on his back, bringing him down to the deck. His friend raised his hand, revealing a long wooden object with tentacle-looking figures at the end. But before he managed to do any damage, he was brought down by another group of women.

Screams emerged from the other side of the wooden barrier, some of pain, others of victory. But I couldn't tell whose were whose.

A door from another section of the ship sprang open as a handful of armed men piled out, yielding weapons of various varieties. Their arms swung with such force that the impact was devastating.

The captives tried to continue their forward movement, but their weak bare fists were no match for the deadly weapons. A mistimed punch was met with a barrage of counterattacks. Blood flowed against the wooden deck and this surprising revolt soon became a sorrowful massacre.

As I finally got to my feet, one of the armed men approached, his weapon at the ready. His weapon barrelled down on me, throwing me back down to the splinter-filled surface. I gripped my bloodied arm as I stared up in horror.

The man raised his arm for the final strike as a young teen threw herself on his back, ripping his neck with her teeth. He screeched out in pain as her grip tightened.

Another woman joined and used the man's weapon against him. Soon, she was joined by men who climbed the barrier, launching a vengeful attack.

My guardian angel stood, blood dripping from her mouth. Her braids covered her face as she looked at her downed opponent. When she raised her head, her soft grey eyes met mine.

I gasped at the sight of her. It was my stalker. Her face was familiar, like I had seen her before outside of the "episodes" but I couldn't place it. Her eyes shined like the freshest silvers. But again, I couldn't place her.

She quickly advanced and knelt by my side. Her hands reached for my wrist and she pulled me into her. I jerked back.

But before she could speak, I slipped into the darkness as my body jerked forward and back.

CHAPTER 28

WHEN REALITY AWOKE, MY eyes shot open and I found myself back in my soft pink chair. Except for this time, I returned to prying eyes, examining my every move.

"Bubble Gum, you, okay?" Madea asked. My glaze was cloudy as I searched the room, eyes flipping from one object to another. I wasn't looking for the girl, but I was at the same time.

"Miracle," Madea said with a raised voice. It wasn't quite yelling, but it might as well have been. I jumped at her words and my eyes met hers.

I slowly stood up and then walked to the bed. As I approached, her hand massaged the base of her neck while her head flinched back.

I extended my hand, but it wasn't towards Madea. Instead, my hand wrapped around the black and white image resting on the picture frame. I picked up the picture and stared.

"Who is this again?" I asked.

"Girl, what is going on with you?"

"Madea!" My tone was not what I intended. Her eyes shot up and she screwed her face. But she didn't yell; no grandmotherly threats.

She gently grasped the picture with pursed lips, treating it like a relic that could crumble with too much pressure. She glared into my eyes for a moment before looking down. Then, her posture softened.

"Dot Jean. My sister."

My eyes scanned the room, but in reality, my mind was going a mile a minute. The girl following me was Madea's sister. It didn't make sense. What did she want from me?

"How did she die?" I asked, no subtly in my tone.

"She's not dead," Madea said.

"Wait, you said she was gone before."

Madea reached for my hand and led me to the bed.

"Bubble Gum, my sister is very much alive. But her mind is gone. It's been that way for as long as I can remember."

My shoulders slumped.

"What happened?" I asked.

She let out an audible sigh and stared at the picture again. A smile crossed her face as her thumb combed over her sister's image.

"You remind me of her. I think that's why you were always my favorite."

I smiled.

"Don't tell your cousins I said that, though."

I nodded.

"Well, she was around your age when it started. At first, it was little things like she'd stare off as if dancing with the clouds. We'd call her name, but it'd take her a few moments to respond. Then came the tremors."

"Tremors?" I asked.

She held up her hands in the air. Her hands were sprinkled with large dark spots accessorized by deep wrinkles and a few scars. As she extended her fingers, my eyes noticed a slight shake.

"You see how my hands shake?"

"Yes, Ma'am," I said.

"Mine does that because God has blessed me with a long life. Hers would shake for no reason at all."

I hid my hands under my legs, hoping she wouldn't notice my tremors.

"Then, other stuff happened; nose bleeds a few times. What scared me was when she'd come back from her daydreams, her breathing was like she'd been drowning for days. Like her lungs were gasping for air, even though she'd be sitting right next to you the whole time. It scared me half to death."

Madea began rocking back and forth from the vivid memories. Her head nodded as she tried to kick the thoughts out of her mind.

"Then what?" I asked. Her eyes met mine again and she continued.

"One day, she never stopped daydreaming." A single tear slid down her cheek. "It was the worse day of my life."

"Where is she now?"

She wiped the tear away and took a deep breath.

"She's at Riverview. You know that one hospital. I visit her every week. This will be the first time I miss a week in…." She stopped to think. Her eyes reached for the ceiling. "I think this will be the first week I ever missed." The realization sank in and I could see the heartbreak in her.

"Go back, Madea. I'll be fine. She needs you. She needs you there more than me." She laced her fingers in mine and squeezed. I covered my other hand over hers as she nodded.

"You're going to be alright, Bubble Gum. You come from a long line of fighters. It's in your bloodline and nothing, and I mean nothing, will ever take that away from you. You hear me? Nothing!" Her tone was powerful.

We embraced in each other's arms. A calm feeling rushed over me, but unfortunately, it didn't last long. I had to figure out why I kept seeing Dot Jean and what she wanted from me.

CHAPTER 29

THE FOLLOWING MORNING, I watched as Madea packed her belongings. With a bit of help from me, she purchased a plane ticket online last night. Dad insisted she wait a few days, but she politely declined, saying, "But what if today is the day my sister finally wakes up? I don't want her all alone when that happens." How could my dad object to that sweet gesture, even if it was far-fetched?

I sank into my chair in the back of the car as my dad drove us to the Los Angeles Airport. I leaned against the window as I watched our beloved city go by.

Some buildings had been restored since the riots that followed Dre's death. But the majority never returned. The fires spread too fast and caused too much damage to salvage. Owners opted to restart their lives elsewhere. Who could blame them? Why support a city when the residents don't even respect your business during challenging times? I get it.

Exhausted from the whirlwind of emotions, I allowed myself not to worry about Dot Jean or finding Ashley or anything else. I let out a deep breath and pressed play on my phone. My eyes glanced over at Madea, whose smile gleamed from ear to ear.

Willow Marie's voice began serenading me; I looked out the window again. A smooth melody emerged as violins caressed the beat. Then, our car disappeared, replaced by another world filled with the absence of light.

The world's beauty shined through the darkness and I was again on steady ground. My eyes were instantly drawn to the maroon-colored walls lined with gold stripes. Flyers for after-school programs flapped against the bulletin board as a soft autumn wind flowed through the air. The smell of excessive perfumes and body sprays contaminated the air, sending a burning sensation through my nostrils.

I was back at school, but this didn't make any sense. Why was I here? Was there a glitch or something in my time machine brain? Oh my God, I just said time machine brain. I am spending too much time with Greg.

I turned to look around and nearly collapsed to my knees. There he was again. Dre.

His feet bounced against the pavement, brushing against other students, but he didn't stop. His eyes were crazed with anger.

Suddenly, Dre shoved Erik to the ground, sending his sandwich flying. A gasp escaped his mouth as he flung himself to the floor.

While his brother watched Erik plummet to the ground, Dre's forearm pressed against the boy's neck, slamming him into the locker behind him. Shock swept over his face and his eyes looked down at his attacker, my brother. The sound of oohs and ahhhs erupted nearby, adding to the hectic scene.

I moved closer but still tried to go unseen.

"What did you do to her, Kurt?" Dre screamed.

Kurt's forearm jerked forward as Dre pressed his weight against Kurt.

"Tell me!" Dre's voice was stern. He was obsessed with rage.

Kurt gasped, trying to breathe despite being constrained.

Dre's body jerked to the left as foreign hands pushed against him. It was Erik. I stepped forward to intervene as Dre stumbled a little but quickly recovered. I stopped moving forward and ducked behind a group of students, pointing their phones at my brother.

"What the hell do you—" Erik started.

Dre's hand flew through the air, finding the center of Erik's chin. His knees wobbled and his body dropped instantly.

Dre turned back to Kurt, whose eyes were focused on Erik, but then he turned to my brother. His eyes widened, his jaw lowered, and Dre's fist flew through the air again.

My brother's body jerked back again, inches from Kurt's chin. This time, it was Mr. Haywood, the English teacher.

"Andre! That is enough," he commanded.

Dre's eyes locked on Kurt. Kurt regained his balanced, wiping blood from his nose, and then shot Dre a devilish smile.

I have never seen Dre act like this, but that smile…the evil smile must have flipped a switch within Dre because he broke away from Mr. Haywood with quickness and charged Kurt. Kurt's body slammed against the locker as Dre's fists flew, connecting to every inch of the no-longer-smiling face.

Kurt attempted to fight back, but he was no match. I was grateful that my dad had taught us how to fight in times like this.

Mr. Haywood and a school security guard had to drag my brother off of Kurt. Blood gushed from his nose and his eye had already swelled.

Camera phones waved in the air, recording every moment of the fight. It wasn't a fight; at least, it was not a fair fight. I knew that, but honestly, I couldn't care less at the time.

My body was flung to the ground, splashing into a dark abyss. Silence echoed throughout the darkness as my soul reached out to find something, anything.

CHAPTER 30

MY BODY ROCKED BACK and forth when I awoke like I was in a moving vehicle. I could hear the clicking of a turn signal, gears being shifted, and finally, the sound of a radio.

> "...*I need a one dance*
> *Got a Hennessy in my hand*
> *One more time 'fore I go*
> *Higher powers taking a hold on me*"

"That was the homie, Drake, doing his thing with *One Dance*. Welcome back to Big Boy's Neighborhood."

A chime rang through the speakers.

"It is my honor. My pleasure to hang out with this dude. We have the one and only Chris Tucker—"

Click

The car had stopped.

My eyes squeezed apart, but the darkness fought me. After several seconds of trying to pry my eyes open, the daylight finally broke free. That had never happened before. I feared this was what Dot Jean might have gone through in her final days.

The world regained its light as I found myself in the back of my mom's car. Dre sat beside her. Our car was parked next to a large green dumpster. Flies buzzed around the overflowing black trash bags as a mixture of French fries and garbage clung to the air. I looked to the left and realized we were in the Jack-in-the-Box parking lot.

"Dre? Mom?" I said, but they didn't answer. They couldn't hear me.

Dre looked down at his hands. Dried-up blood tattooed his throbbing knuckles. My mom sat silent, which was never a good sign. Her knuckles were practically white as they gripped the steering wheel.

Her head faced forward, but her eyes screamed with anger. She clenched her jaw and the little vein on her neck echoed the sentiment.

Dre kept his head down, massaging his hands. My mom let out an audible sigh.

"Do you want to explain why a busted-up little boy is in the nurse's office right now, Dre?"

"I—" he started.

"Boy, we taught you to look at someone when speaking to them, so you'd better look at me," she commanded.

He lifted his head and met her eyes.

"I think," he stuttered. Dre sighed. "I think he did something to Ashley."

"*Did* something? Dre, what are you talking about? What did he do?" Her voice was elevated.

His head went down again as I leaned forward.

"Dre," she said.

His eyes met hers once again.

"I think he…," more stuttering, "abused her. Like…" His lip began to quiver as his eyes faded off in the distance. Her stone expression slowly faded away. She finally understood.

"Oh," she said. Her voice was softer now. And then, she lowered her head, staring into her lap. Her eyes flung from right to left and back again, trying to find the words to tell her son.

Most moms would comfort their children. Tell them it'll be okay and monsters like that will get what they deserve. Tell them something to make their child feel better, even if it is a lie. My mom wasn't like that.

Showing emotions wasn't easy for her. She was taught to be a tough Black woman. Don't let anyone hold you back or say you can't do anything. Sometimes you shove your feelings and emotions to the side and wear your own mask; because warriors and fighters are in your bloodline. That is how she survived.

After a minute or so, she pushed the key back into the ignition.

My body jerked as pounding emerged from the window. It was Dot Jean. My eyes widened. My hand flung to my mouth, shielding a scream.

With a pained stare, her fist flew to the window again. I turned to the front of the car, but my mom and Dre both just sat there, unaware of the manic scene in the back. They couldn't see or hear her.

Her eyes bore into my soul as she raised another fist. Her arm stretched back as her fist hung in the air.

"What do you want!" I screamed.

Her hand slowly lowered. She leaned forward and placed her spread palm against the window.

The world seemed unusually quiet as two time-travelers stared into each other's eyes. She lowered her head. Her body seemed to collapse in despair.

The fight drained out of her while her spirit shrunk into almost nothing. I swallowed and placed my hand opposite hers. With my other hand, I gently tapped against the window, raising her attention. Her head popped up.

Her eyes went to my hand, then to my face. I nodded and she reflected my actions. We both lowered our hands. Her lips opened and she began to speak. But the window served as an impenetrable barrier, making her words muted.

I shrugged.

"I can't hear you," I said.

She looked around in desperation, trying to find something nearby.

My mom turned the keys in the ignition and the car revved up. Dot Jean noticed my reaction. We were running out of time. She clenched her fist and slammed one against the window.

I jerked back, which resulted in her hands waving in the air. Maybe as an apology. Then, her eyes popped up. She leaned forward; her face stood inches away from the window.

Her mouth widened as she breathed against the window until a medium-sized circle appeared. With her pointer finger, she carefully wrote. My heart dropped as I read her message: HELP HER!

"Help who?" I screamed. I pounded on the window. My hand flung to the doorknob, but it wouldn't open. When I looked back up, the girl was gone.

"Who was I supposed to help?" I thought. I growled and clenched my fist. Who was I supposed to help? I leaned against the window, racking my brain for an answer.

"Don't tell Miracle." My mom's words broke my train of thought.

"Do you hear me?" she asked. "Do not tell your sister." Dre nodded.

"Ashley!" I said. But Ashley was a ghost. No one has seen or heard from her. It couldn't be her. My mind zipped from one thought to another. Then, my eyes shot up with the realization of who she was. My lips parted and my soul collapsed forward, diving into a pool of darkness. The silent waves crashed against my inner being as once again I was alone in the vast blackness.

CHAPTER 31

MY EYES SHOT OPEN and I quickly reached for my phone, then stopped. We were already back home. But, a second ago, we were in the car.

"Did we already drop Madea off?" I asked.

My dad stared blankly at me and scratched his cheek.

"Um…You okay, Bubble Gum? We've been back for a few hours."

I didn't respond. Instead, I jumped from the couch and headed to the bedroom.

"Miracle?" My dad's voice rang throughout the hallway, but still, I ignored him.

The phone rang several times. Each ring felt like a lifetime. Finally, someone picked up.

"Hey, it's me…Miracle. Whatever you do, do not hang out with Erik. Trust me; he's bad news. Carry a weapon or something. Just stay away. Do you understand me? Kim?"

There was a long pause. Her breathing filled the airway. Then, she spoke.

"It's too late."

Click.

I stared at the phone. The trembling in my hands grew erratic. I slid the phone into my pocket and ran out the door.

"I'll be back. Gotta go to Kim's," I yelled as the front door slammed behind me.

I leaped up her steps, taking two at a time, and then rapidly beat my fist against her door. I panted furiously as I waited. Light broke free from her window, so I knew someone was home.

The door slowly opened and her father stood there. His red-filled eyes widened when he saw me, but his face quickly softened. We stood there for a moment, not saying a word, then he stepped to the side, opening the door to invite me in.

The smell of jalapenos danced in the air. It always smelled like that when he made his famous beef fajitas. Those were Kim's favorite.

"I missed his cooking," I thought as I rounded the corner to her bedroom.

I pushed the door open, revealing a world that used to be my second home. It hadn't changed. Her BTS poster still hung on the opposite wall and her pink faux chair that matched mine sat underneath.

A black bookshelf stood alongside her dresser, filled with a wide assortment of books. Her collection of Harry Potter books sat next to Alex Cross, which leaned against John Grimson's Theodore Boone.

My eyes move to her bed where she lay. Her body, partially covered by a blanket, faced away from the door. I slowly walked towards her and sat beside her, the bed creaking slightly.

I reached for her but stopped in the air. My hand hovered above her, then softly landed against her skin. She was warm. I tried pulling her towards me, but she resisted.

I leaned down. My lips were inches from her ear.

"Kim," I whispered.

She sighed and turned.

My eyes grew wide and I gasped. Her face was a battered version of the beautiful girl I once knew. The white of one eye was spray-painted red, while her lip was busted. Scars marked her chin.

My heart sank. I should have been there for her. She was the perfect target for Erik. All alone because the world abandoned her, labeling her as a snitch or traitor. I could only imagine what else she had gone through.

Without thinking, my body collapsed over her, embracing her. Our tears merged as we shared the same heartbreak, the same pain, the same fear. For that brief moment, we were sisters again.

We held each other for hours. Eventually, we both fell asleep, her shoulder as my pillow. She'd wake a few times, rattled by nightmares. I'd rub her back until she drifted off again.

CHAPTER 32

THE FOLLOWING MORNING, OUR hands were locked as the glass door opened. We stepped into the building and my heart pounded like never before. The distinct smell of coffee and a musty aroma floated in the air.

My eyes blinked rapidly as I took deep breaths and we walked forward. An older man stared at us from behind the front desk. His eyes scanned us both up and down and a grimace spread across his face. We stepped forward.

"How may I help you?" he asked. His voice was gruff, not the welcoming voice you'd expect once you walked into the building.

Kim stood there, head down, arms folded. Every sound made her jump. She squeezed my hand.

"I got this, Terry," a man's voice blasted from our side. I noticed the scar over his eyebrow first.

"Glad you came in." He extended his hand to Kim, who avoided eye contact. She turned to me. Our eyes met and I gave her a nod. She raised her hand and they shook.

"I'll do everything I can to help," he said. His voice was softer than what I remembered … trusting, actually. We proceeded to the backroom.

He opened the door for us and Kim stepped in. I hesitated. This room held too many painful memories. My chest heaved up and down as each question replayed in my head: "Was Dre a gang member? Did Rieko give Dre the gun?" And worst of all, "why did Andre point the gun at the officers?"

"Are you okay?" he asked, breaking the horror movie replaying in my mind. I looked at Kim, who was already sitting at the table. I couldn't leave her behind. As Madea said, my bloodline was filled with fighters and I needed to fight. I exhaled and stepped in.

The interview lasted maybe thirty to forty minutes. It started with us being introduced to SVU Detective Myers, the female detective running point on our case. Officer Wright swore she was the best and she wanted to help.

Kim replayed the entire story of her attack, including the first time he approached her alone.

"It was after school. He began rubbing the back of my elbow, saying, 'you have no one else. You should just hang with me and Jake.'" She rubbed her elbow as if it still burned from his touch. Then, she continued.

"I stepped back and slapped him. I was so mad. I ran to the bus. I didn't know what he was going to do to me. That's when I saw you," she paused and looked at me.

Oh my God. That day she climbed on the bus after I saw her and Erik. That's the day she was talking about. Her face wasn't red from embarrassment. It was red from anger.

"I wanted to tell you then, but," she paused, "I didn't think you'd care."

I squeezed her hand. Tears rolled down my cheeks, splashing onto the floor. Watching Kim go through this was hard. Her chin shivered, tears streamed down her cheek, and she looked to the walls for answers.

Detective Myers was patient and allowed Kim to continue only when ready. Kim swallowed and began.

"I had just left my apartment, trying to clear my head. Nights were the hardest for me since they felt the loneliest. So lately, I've been taking walks. When I went around the side of the complex, I noticed this guy leaning on a beat-up brown truck. He wore a hoody, so I didn't realize who it was. I didn't think anything of it.

When I was about to pass him, he reached out and grabbed me," she winced as if she was reliving the moment. "I tried to shake him off, but he was too strong. He must have punched me or something because it felt like my face smacked into a brick wall and my knees buckled.

He pulled me into the truck. I tried to push him away, but he kept hitting me. All I could do was block. I…I tried to scream but stopped when I felt," she paused as her fingers fidgeted underneath the table, "when I felt the knife pressed against my neck."

My hand moved to my mouth as I squeezed her hand tighter.

"Then, I heard it. His voice." Kim's face scrunched in disgust.

"I could see him smiling under the hood. That freaking smile," she nodded her head.

"I could feel him touching me. Sliding his hand in…" she paused for a moment. I shot Detective Myers a glance and she did the same to me.

"My body just went numb. I stared out the window into the night sky. There were no stars out, just birds flying by. Nine."

"I'm sorry. Nine what?" Detective Myers asked.

"Nine birds. It took nine birds to fly by before he finished." A dreadful silence lingered in the room. Her hand released mine and her shoulders slumped. I just stared into her beautiful eyes, which poured tears of pain. She didn't deserve this. No one deserves this.

Kim finally broke the silence.

"I'm not sure how long it lasted, but when he was done…when he was done, he leaned down and whispered, 'thank you.' He thanked me." Her lips quivered, matching the rest of her body. She slumped down, leaning onto the table. Her cries screamed out, echoing in the room.

"I should have fought more; maybe this wouldn't—"

Detective Myers reached out her hand, grabbing onto Kim's.

"You did the best thing possible, Kim. You survived."

I let Detective Myers' words sink in. "You survived." She was right. It could have been a lot worse. The horrors Kim had gone through seemed unreal.

After the interview, Kim and her dad dropped me back at home. When I walked in, I folded myself into my dad's arms. His heartbeat comforted me as my tears stained his t-shirt. I sobbed in his arms, and reality finally set in. Life was hard and it didn't wait until high school was over.

CHAPTER 33

MY FEET POUNDED THE pavement while my arms sliced through the air. My hips were forward and my elbows were closed. My form was perfect. With every step, my lungs expanded and deflated on cue. I was in my element.

My earbuds snuggly blasted CyHi the Prince's song, *Mandela*. The tribal beat pounded against my heart as my soul enjoyed the ride.

The brisk kiss of the wind brushed my cheeks as trees waved me on. I rounded the corner to my apartment complex and picked up the pace. My stride extended and my heart raced, allowing my body to take control.

I slowed my pace to a fast walk, helping my lungs and heart recover. I tilted my head up and took focused breaths. My hands rested on my hips which already ached.

I stood there, catching my breath as I looked at the clouds that circled above. A white-winged butterfly with faint black rings glided in the sky, pirouetting for my approval. I stared at the beautiful creature as my music provided the perfect beat for its vibrant dance.

As it soared away, my body tilted forward into the ground, splashing into the abyss. My world was no more and I patiently waited to find where I landed.

CHAPTER 34

AS THE DARKNESS CONSUMED life, the sounds of a piano flowed in the background. Beethoven, maybe. Mozart? I was never the best at classics. But the music was calming.

My eyes opened, revealing a room filled with people, all in white shirts on top of white pants. No logos, no images, just plain white.

A small black tape deck sat in the corner of the room, blaring classical music, which all the people seemed to ignore, except for one elderly lady who held an imaginary partner as her hips swayed from side to side.

A younger woman with curly red hair stood in front of a mirror, yelling at her own reflection. An Asian man stared aimlessly at a blank television set while two men played chess, although neither had the correct pieces. The queen was replaced by two checkers stacked on top of each other. The king was a water bottle top and the rooks didn't even exist.

The other patrons walked like zombies; slight moans escaped their mouths. Their bare feet slid across the tile floor as their bodies lurched forward, not genuinely having a direction or purpose.

As a long-haired woman walked in front of me, two men in navy blue scrubs wrote on their clipboards. The blonde man pointed to the woman.

"She has schizophrenia."

"Oh wow." The other took a step back as she approached.

"No, I don't want to. Shhh, they'll hear you," the woman rambled. Her eyes followed the men as she crouched, wrapping her hands around herself.

The two men moved past the rambling woman to the next person.

"And what about this one?"

"Mike, that's Alvin. Old military vet. Still thinks he's in the war most days. Today's a good day, though."

"Dang. And her?" Mike asked, pointing to a woman sitting in a wheelchair. Her long white hospital gown hung on her frail body. Her curly grey hair flowed down to her midsection and her eyes…her grey eyes stared off into the distance.

"Dot Jean," I mumbled.

I was so used to seeing her teenage version, but there was no denying it. It was her. Her eyes stood frozen in time as her body slumped over. I moved closer to hear the two men.

"That's Dorothy. She's been a vegetable for over 60 years. Maybe 70, I forget. She's harmless. Now this one," he said, pointing to the man in front of the television.

His voice faded as I tiptoed closer to Dot Jean and waved my hand in front of her face. No reaction. Her statued form didn't move. Her chest inflated and then deflated, so at least I knew she was still alive. But her mind was gone.

"Can you hear me?" I whispered. "Dorothy? Dot Jean?" Still nothing. "I'm so sorry. I don't know if you can hear me, but," I paused. My head lowered as I thought of Kim. "I couldn't save her. I'm sorry. I'm so sorry. I was too late."

My hand slid over hers and I squeezed. Her hand was home to slender fingers and bulging veins. Her moles reminded me of the big dipper.

When I squeezed, her body jerked forward as she exhaled deeply. She remained arched as if the air was finding its way back into her lungs. Then she collapsed back in the chair.

I jerked back, stumbling over my legs. I scooted backward on my hands, running into the leg of the table, interrupting the chess game.

"Quit cheating," one man yelled at the other. His opponent sat at the table, eyes barely open and a trickle of drool sliding out of his mouth.

I continued staring at Dot Jean. Her eyes sparkled and then returned to their paralyzed state. I reached out to her, but my vision went black, fading into a familiar darkness.

CHAPTER 35

AS MY BODY PRESSED against a hard surface, my eyes slowly opened, revealing a blurry world. I expected the sun's heat to press against my cheeks while sweat poured down my face. But when my vision returned, my chest tightened.

Stretched in front of me was a long hallway with white blanketing the walls, floor, and ceiling. I stood up. A wave of nausea splashed against my soul. My knees wobbled, so I used the wall to steady myself.

I closed my eyes and took deep, deliberate breaths. After a few seconds, I opened them and stepped forward. I peered down the endless hall. My eyes were drawn to hundreds, maybe thousands of doors pressed firmly against the walls.

They were all identical, looking like standard doors you would find on any cookie-cutter house. Brass door knobs shined, yearning to be turned.

"Hello?" I shouted.

My voice banged against the emptiness, but there were no echoes. Staring off into the distance, I could see no end. The smell of emptiness lingered in the air.

"Hello?" I repeated; still nothing.

With a long sigh, I stepped to the first door, turned the knob, and walked in.

Another long narrow hallway greeted me. Floral wallpaper covered the tan-painted walls. The air smelled like the tile floors had been recently mopped, a mix between a stale mop and bleach.

Stepping forward, I peered out the window. Snow sprinkled the green grass as frost pressed against the window. My eyes examined the background, trying to find any signs or indications of where I was or when.

"Doctor! We need a doctor," a man screamed, pushing a woman in a wheelchair down the hall.

The overhead lights bounced off his glistening forehead. His eyes bulged as his breathing tiptoed on the verge of hyperventilating. I stared at my dad in amazement. It was him, just maybe 15 years younger.

He pushed the wheelchair down the hall. A younger version of my mom sat inside. Her hair puffed in a mini-afro while her turquoise loop earrings bounced erratically. Her cheeks inflated and then sank as her breathing intensified. Sweat poured out while her moans of pain bounced against the walls.

Her eyes squeezed together as she exhaled deeply. My jaw dropped when I looked down. Her hands clung to her enlarged stomach.

Time seemed to slow while I stared at them. A heaviness sank inside me, realizing she was about to give birth…to me.

My mom often told me stories of my birth. How her water broke 11 days earlier than expected and how they almost died getting to the hospital. That cold Wednesday afternoon was filled with freezing temperatures and slick roads due to the unusual snowfall.

It wasn't every day it snowed in Lancaster. In fact, it hardly ever snowed. My dad said the snow was a miracle, but my mom confessed that surviving my father's driving was the miracle.

I pressed myself to the wall as they sprinted by and rounded the corner. Without thinking, I turned and followed. But as I did, my body jerked back into the white hallway, the door slamming behind me.

"No," I screamed, pounding on the door. I jiggled the knob, but it was locked. My fist slammed against the door but was met with only a painful hand.

I pressed my back against the door and slid down.

"Hello," I screamed. "Where am I?"

With every question, my head banged against the door.

"How do I get out of here?"

Bang

"Can anyone hear me?"

Bang

My mind raced as my head slumped between my legs. All of my thoughts seem to smother me at once. My chest tightened and I struggled to breathe. A single tear ran down my cheek.

I sat there for a while, letting the silence shield me from my thoughts. Each thought brought about another question. Each question came with the awful realization that I was stuck in an endless cycle of memories and ghosts.

"Get it together, girl," I reprimanded myself.

"What should I do? What should I do?" I repeated.

My head pressed against the door. I closed my eyes and took deep, deliberate breaths.

As my lungs deflated, my heart slowed and the tightening sensation in my chest decreased. I opened my eyes and turned down the hallway. The answer was right in front of me the entire time.

"Find my way home. To do that, I have to find the right door."

There was nothing here to help. I had to figure this out on my own. I stood up and moved to the next door.

"Wait. There *was* someone who could help." My eyes perked up. "I have to find Dot Jean!"

With that, I turned the knob and walked inside.

CHAPTER 36

AFTER THREE MORE ATTEMPTS, I was back in the white hallway. I moved to the next door. Sighing in frustration, I stared down at the knob.

As I twisted my wrist, a soft whimper floated in my ears. I peered down the hall and my jaw dropped. There she was.

She sat against the wall, curled into a little ball. Her head pressed against her forearms. I approached slowly. I didn't know how she would react seeing me and I didn't want her to run.

"Hello?" My voice was soft, less threatening and more confused.

Her head popped up and her beautiful grey eyes rested on mine. Her mouth opened as she stood up.

"Hi," I said.

I stretched out my arms, revealing open palms. She stared at them like she'd never seen hands before.

"How did you get here?" she asked. "You have to leave. You have to go back."

"I can't. I don't know how," I shrugged.

Her eyes bounced around my shoulder, looking for something or someone.

"How did you get *here*? In *this* room." She tilted her head and inched closer.

"The door," I shrugged again.

"Where's the door? Show me!"

"This way, I can—"

She snatched my wrist before I could finish and pulled me down the hall. I gasped at the shock.

"Where is it? Where?" Her questions quickly turned to yells.

"Just up here." Our feet pounded against the white floor for a few minutes until our breathing grew shallow.

"Wait. It should be here." My head flipped through the hallway. "I didn't walk that far to get to you. It should be right here."

My heart pounded as I wrenched my neck, looking down the hall. Each door looked the same as the next.

"Where is it?" Now I was shouting.

I turned to her. Her shoulders dropped and a streak of pain flashed over her face. She let out an exhaustive breath and stared at the floor.

"It's gone," she mumbled.

"I swear it was right here," I pleaded. "It was right here!"

She pressed her back against the wall, sliding down to her original position.

"You're stuck," she paused, "like me."

"No, there has to be a way out. What's at the end of the hallway?"

"Nothing. It doesn't end. It never ends." Her voice grew soft, timid even.

I stood opposite her and collapsed against the facing wall. A restless silence hung between us as my mind reached for answers.

"How long have you been here?" I asked.

"A few days. A few months. No clue. Time works differently here." She turned her head to face down the hallway. Her sighs were heavy.

My eyes examined her 13-year-old body. I didn't have the heart to confess she was over 80 years old. She should look like Madea, but instead, she looked like a younger version of me.

"Have you always been alone?" I asked.

"No, there was a man here. Sylvester. He was here before me."

My head popped up.

"Wait, before you? Where is he now?"

"He's not here. He's…um, gone."

"Like he's in one of the rooms?" I asked, looking at the various doors.

"No," she said. Her answer hung between us for a while.

"Do you know why we are here?" I asked.

She shook her head.

"I think we're supposed to change things in the future, maybe." Her words squeezed between her squished cheeks while her face pressed against her forearms.

"Have you changed anything?"

She lifted her head. Her eyebrows clenched together as she looked up.

"Not sure. Wouldn't know if I did."

"Yeah, I guess."

My body slumped. Dot Jean didn't have any more answers than I had. Defeat poured out of her. The strong-spirited girl who chased me was no more, replaced by someone defeated.

"This will not happen to me," I thought. I pressed one hand against the wall and pulled myself up.

"Where are you going?" she asked. Her words had slowed.

"One of these doors has the answer. I'm going to find it."

"But I've tried almost every door and I'm still here."

"I know. But I can't give up. I have to fight. Come with me." I reached out my hand, but she stared at it briefly and waved me off.

"I'm tired." She repositioned her body and spread across the floor.

I stood over her for a moment. Her eyes closed and for once, she looked at peace. I nodded and walked away. I was determined to try every door if I had to. I refused to be like her. I refused to give up hope. Madea told me there were fighters in my bloodline and now was the time to fight.

CHAPTER 37

A THUNDEROUS ROAR STRETCHED through the air as exhaust fumes floated from the motorcycles. Rows of bikers lined the streets, inching forward. Their boots pressed against the burning pavement, steadying their motorcycles as large American flags waved from the rear.

People lined the sidewalks, waving and cheering on the riders. Children clung to their parents' legs as oversized headphones protected their small ear drums.

I covered my ears, but my hands were no match for the gigantic roar of the metal dragons. The motorcycles revved slowly. The line moved forward as one biker morphed into another and then another. One bike appeared as soon as the first one stretched down the road.

A man in a U.S. Marine uniform stood in the middle of the street. His shaky fingers pressed tightly against each other as he saluted every motorcycle. Sweat beaded down his face as a slight pain oozed over his clean-shaven face. He only broke his position to hug motorcyclists who stopped and offered a show of gratitude.

My eyes traced back to the riders and I sucked in a quick breath as my hand moved to my mouth. From the sidewalk, I saw a younger version of my dad appear. His legs straddled a slick black motorcycle; two large silver pipes extended from the side. He wore one of those half helmets and a motorcycle vest covered in military insignias. Ribbons jingled as he rode past.

A gleam set in his eyes and his smile stretched from ear to ear. With a twist of his wrist, his motorcycle came alive again, singing its own beautiful melody. He extended a hand to the crowd as two flags waved behind him; one was the American flag, with bright reds, blues, and whites, and the other was black with a silhouetted face.

My teeth-filled smile followed his path and any tension held within me was gone. My palms slammed against each other, joining in with the mesmerized crowd. And then…my body jerked back into my prison of white.

I stared at the doorknob and smiled at the thought of my dad. When I turned to Dot Jean, she was gone.

"Hello?" I screamed, but my words trailed off into the abyss.

Dot Jean never returned. Her void was filled with a chilling silence. I used the past within these doors to serve as my only companion.

I wasn't sure how long I had been trapped in this world. Dot Jean said time worked differently here. Maybe one door was an hour; perhaps it was a year. Or maybe…

Each door drove me through a world of emotion. Door 11 plunged me into my family's birth with my parents' wedding day.

I watched my parents slide a slice of lemon into their mouths. Their faces scrunched up instantly. According to the preacher, lemon represented the sourness and hardship of marriage. But as sourness from a lemon quickly dissipates, so too would the difficulties of marriage. All you need is patience and endurance.

The next taste came from a clear liquid; vinegar. Again, their faces scrunched up. My dad extended his tongue as his taste buds reacted. The bitterness of the vinegar was weaker than the lemon and represented the minor issues that may arise in marriage.

Then, they lifted a small bowl filled with a burnt brown substance. They dipped their fingers inside and nearly jumped from the reaction. Cayenne pepper represented passion within the marriage. Both physical and mental.

Finally, they tasted the last item, honey. The sweetness of the honey represented everything desired in marriage. It expressed the joy and beauty that was to follow. People in the crowd cried. I cried.

CHAPTER 38

DOOR 59 WAS QUITE the opposite. A malnourished little girl named Darlene sat cross-legged inside a locked closet. Flies buzzed around her head as her only light source crept from under the door frame. Darlene's father, who smelled of booze and regret, slumped onto a chair in the tiny living room, a cigarette dangling from his fingertips.

In door 68, I learned Darlene's mother died giving birth to her; what was supposed to be a joyful occasion buried this man into an overpowering world of pain. He blamed Darlene.

His pain drove him to alcohol. This pain intertwined with his soul so much that he couldn't see the talented angel standing before him. Instead, the demons within him transformed him into something else.

As Darlene curled herself into a ball, her soft young voice reached for the stars. Her voice was so powerful, even at a young age. Although she couldn't see or hear me, I knelt beside her, hoping she could feel my presence. Her world reminded me a lot of mine.

I closed the door behind me; door 123. My hand slid off the doorknob and went limp. I stood at the door and stared. A long, low sigh escaped my lips. I stumbled a bit. My hand reached for the wall, but my body collapsed to the floor as my knees gave out.

Unparalleled mental fatigue rushed over me as the stark reality of being trapped (physically and mentally) rested on my soul. A quivering breath flew through the air.

I laid against the white floor. My breathing slowed and my eyelids soon drifted.

"I'll just rest for a minute," I told myself. "Just for a minute. I'm so tired."

The fighter inside me needed to rest. It needed a moment to breathe. I closed my eyes and let the darkness take over.

CHAPTER 39

A SPARK OF FIRE emerged as the fighter within me came alive once more. I opened my eyes and looked upon the vast white hall. My squished cheeks peeled away from the floor, and I staggered to my feet. My body felt heavy and every movement forced me on the verge of collapsing where I stood. But still, I stepped forward.

I staggered down the hall, the wall acting as a supportive friend. When I blinked, I had to force my eyes open. Each step felt like a mile and each mile wore on my tired soul. I would give anything to be back in my bedroom on the hard floor with Madea's CPAP machine serenading me sounds of the ocean.

I swallowed hard as I flung my body onto a shut door. My face pressed against its cool surface. My hand slid down, finding the doorknob. I squeezed tightly, fearing I'd become one with the floor once again. With a twist, it opened and I stepped inside. My heart froze.

When I emerged from the emptiness, I found myself back home. A lightness filled my chest. My heart pulsed rapidly as I stared at my dad sitting at the table. His marble brown eyes stared at his beautiful wife, who rolled her eyes in his direction. Dre sat beside them, shoveling macaroni and cheese into his already full mouth. My breath escaped me.

"Dre," I shrieked.

He brought the fork to his mouth, oblivious to my words.

My heart sank upon the realization this was just another dream…another episode. My stomach tightened as a wave of nausea set in. My disappointment was interrupted by a fist pounding on the door.

Boom Boom

"I got it," Dre said. As he barrelled by me, I reached out for him. My hand slid between his body as if he didn't exist…or I didn't.

Once Dre opened the door, he was greeted by Mr. Simmons. His steely eyes looked over Dre while a salt and pepper goatee framed his clenched lips.

"Hey, Mr.—"

"Andre, you have to stop writing my daughter." His voice was stern, cold with anger.

My parents approached the door, opening it wider.

"Jackson, what's going on?" my mom asked.

"Hey, Jackson," my dad said. His tone was weird like it was filled with sadness.

Mr. Simmons broke his stare and glanced up at my parents. Then back at Dre. He lowered his head, letting out an audible sigh.

"Andre here keeps writing Ashley letters and I," he paused. He lifted a plastic bag from his side. His grip screamed frustration. "It needs to stop."

My mom placed her hand on Dre's shoulder, but Dre didn't turn to look. Instead, his eyes were glued to the bag.

"I just thought—," he began.

"It. Needs. To. Stop." Mr. Simmons' voice cracked.

"It will," my mom said.

Through the foggy material, I could see unopened envelopes and they all appeared to be from Dre to Ashley.

"It will," my mom repeated, staring at her precious son. Her eyes read worry and concern.

Mr. Simmons turned to walk away and then stopped. He looked over his shoulder and said, "she's not going to write you back."

My mom slowly closed the door, and her eyes again blanketed her son. Dre stood motionless, staring at the door as if he was waiting for Mr. Simmons' words to disappear from existence, but they didn't.

A single tear trickled down Dre's cheek. His chest heaved up and down while his eyes slammed shut. His head dropped and the single tear soon morphed into a river of sadness.

"You, okay?" My mom leaned into him.

My dad glanced at my mom and then stepped back. Maybe he was unsure how to comfort his son or just knew my mom was what Dre needed. Either way, my mom wrapped her arms around Dre, squeezing him tightly.

It was weird to watch. My mom and Dre were always close, but she never babied Dre or me. She raised us to be strong-willed and fighters because that was how her parents raised her.

Don't get me wrong, my mom loved us, and we knew it, but saying "I love you" wasn't her specialty. She said it in other ways. Dre and I understood that. To have her wrap her arms around my brother and embrace him shocked me. But I was grateful for it; I was jealous I couldn't comfort him too.

Dre fell into my mom's arms and cried. His tears flowed like Autumn rain. I turned to my dad, who hid his own tears.

After a few minutes, Dre assured my mom he was alright. I knew she didn't believe him, but I didn't think she knew how to handle her firstborn's broken heart. He gave my mom one last hug and nodded to my dad.

"I just want to be alone right now, if that's okay." His voice was calm, even.

They both nodded.

"Yeah, that's fine," my dad said.

Dre looked them both in the eyes, examining them. With a deep sigh, he walked past them and headed to his room. I followed. When he opened his bedroom door, I squeezed in before he could close it, but my body jerked forward, collapsing into a still void.

My arms and legs hung in the air as a familiar feeling of falling rushed over me. My eyes open to find a pool of darkness covering me. I had missed the falling sensation.

"Wait," I thought. *"Did this mean I was...."*

CHAPTER 40

MY CHEST HEAVED TOWARD the stars, suspending itself in mid-air. I gasped while air slowly leaked into my lungs. After several seconds, my body collapsed onto the warm surface. Faint beeping emerged as soft murmurs intertwined near my feet. My head flopped from one side to the other, occasionally lifting just to be pulled down by the force of gravity.

My eyelids were heavy and every attempt to open them came with strain and force. I continued to struggle as moans escaped my lips. My left eye slightly opened, then my right. Together they revealed an unfamiliar world covered in a blanket of blurriness.

More garbled speech came from the blobs who approached. My head flopped against the surface as I tried to regain my strength to run, or evade, or whatever I needed to do to survive. As the world regained focus, a beaming light wrapped me in its embrace, sending my eyes back into the darkness.

I felt soft fingertips slide across my hand. I struggled to turn my head and face the blob who sat mere inches away. My eyes set upon my hand and stared as the mass continued to massage my skin.

The figure gradually turned into skinny sand-colored fingers stretched from a slender forearm. Then, it shifted, transforming into a young woman. Her deep-set ocean eyes glistened behind her transparent framed glasses.

My eyelids stood heavy as my eyes squished together, adjusting my vision to see clearer. Her face was focused on her hand sliding across mine. She hummed a sweet melody that collided with numerous beeps and alarms that chirped from my other side.

Too weak to turn my head, I focused on her.

"Hello." At least, that was what I tried to say. Instead, my words were drowned by garbled moans and a trickle of drool, which clung to my chin.

"Miracle," a soft voice whispered, "you're safe now."

Someone clenched onto my right hand on my other side, squeezing it between theirs. With every amount of energy, I turned my head and saw my dad sitting next to me. His tears dripped onto my hand. His body trembled with every breath.

"Doctor," he bellowed. "Doctor!"

"Doctor?" I thought, *"Was I in a hospital?"*

The world slowly faded as a stocky Latina walked into the room. Her medical badges jingled against her chest. I tried to speak again, but the weight of my eyelids became too much. I faded back into the darkness.

CHAPTER 41

THE DISTINCT SMELL OF bleach splashed against my nose. My head pounded with every beep and boop from nearby machines. I leaned forward, but hands gently pressed against my shoulders.

"No, no. Take it easy. You're okay."

My dad hovered over me as his sweet smile greeted me. I reached out my hand to him, but my arms were constrained by wires and tubes everywhere. An IV was glued to my arm as a tube ran from a large transparent bag, holding a clear substance inside.

On the other side of me, wires ran to a portable display of what I assumed were my vital signs. Several beeps emerged from the machine as numbers rose and then dropped.

"Dad," I mumbled, "what happened? Where am I?"

"You're at UCLA hospital. You're safe," he said.

I stared at his hand pressed against mine. This wasn't a dream. It wasn't another episode. This was real. The thought brought tears to my eyes. I sat silent for a moment, letting the realization sink in. I was finally back.

"Kim? Where did she go? I just saw her," I asked.

"That was three days ago. She's at school right now. She only comes on the weekends."

"Three days ago? Wait, how long have I been here?"

He stared at me for a moment and then responded.

"Six months."

His words hit me like a dagger. Six months? Six months? My mind couldn't comprehend what he was telling me. I leaned forward but was too drained and collapsed back on the hospital bed.

"Hey, take it easy. You're back now and that's all that matters."

"Yeah, I was back, but for how long," I thought.

The fresh breeze gently caressed my cheeks as the nurse pushed me through the hospital doors. I closed my eyes and enjoyed the moment. The smell of freshly cut grass floated towards me, while the sound of car tires turning against the hot pavement screeched in the air.

After several days of observations and being poked and prodded, the perplexed hospital staff finally released me. They labeled my case as Neurocardiogenic Syncope or something like that, basically meaning I passed out. I was ordered to return every two weeks for more tests until the doctors could figure out what happened. I was okay with that. I just wanted to get home and return to my everyday life.

"Here you go, Miracle," the nurse said.

"Thank you." I shot her a smile and pushed myself out of the chair, just in time to see my parents pull up along the drop-off area.

"Ready to go home?" my mom asked, opening the car door for me.

"You have no idea," I said, throwing myself into the backseat. "It feels good to be…I don't know, to be awake, I guess."

"We're glad you're back," my mom said.

"I'll second that one," my dad said, shifting the car into drive.

Only an hour's drive until I could finally feel at home again. I missed that feeling.

CHAPTER 42

THE CAR JERKED BACK and forth as L.A. traffic
greeted us on the highway. I peered out the window, grateful
to be out of the hospital and on our way home. I wanted to
return to my old life and see what the last six months had
brought.

"Are you hungry? We can stop and pick up some
burgers or something," my mom said, twisting her body from
the passenger seat.

"No, I'm alright," I said, ripping the medical bracelet
off my wrist.

"Okay." She shot me a smile and then turned back
around.

"I'm just excited to get back home. Ya know?"

"Yeah, we get that," my dad said, looking at me
through the rear-view mirror.

"Anything you want to do?" my mom asked.

"Not really. Maybe see Kim. Greg. Oh, did you already tell Madea? If not, I can video chat with her and surprise her. She probably figured out video chatting by now, right?"

My dad turned to my mom. She nodded and then twisted her body again to face me.

"I'm sorry, baby."

I turned to face her and met her eyes.

"Miracle, while you were gone, Madea passed away."

My heart sank as I let the weight of her words hit me. I felt like I was falling, but my body didn't move.

"No," I said, "no, she was fine a few months ago." I shook my head and waved my hands in the air.

"I'm so sorry," my mom said. She reached out her hand and grabbed mine.

My dad contorted his body and reached his right hand back as well. I could see his arm straining, but he didn't let go.

"But…how?" I stuttered.

"It was peaceful. In her sleep," my mom said gently.

"When?"

There was a brief silence before my mom responded.

"Four months ago."

I squeezed their hands but looked away. The city blurred through my tears. The rest of the ride was filled with awkward silences as memories of Madea floated into my head.

After we got home, I excused myself and went to my room. My mind swirled with thoughts of Madea and how I didn't have the opportunity to say goodbye.

Knock knock

"Sorry about Madea. We were planning on telling you when we got home. Didn't want to bombard you with everything right away."

"It's okay, dad. I'm sorry too," I said. "I can't believe she's gone."

"Yeah, me either." He wrapped his arm around me, pulling me into him.

"What was her funeral like? I bet she had a lot of people there. Everyone loved her."

He didn't respond. Instead, he turned his head away and stared at the floor.

"Dad?"

"I didn't go."

"What? Why not?"

He turned back to me and placed his hand on my back.

"I always knew you were going to wake up. But I just didn't know when. I didn't want you to wake up alone, so," he paused, "I decided not to go so I could be with you when you woke up."

A pained stare rested on his face. He tried to smile, but it was a weak attempt. It didn't fool me. I knew all of this was my fault.

"You didn't get to say goodbye."

"It's okay, Bubble Gum," he said.

"No, it's not." I sat up and turned to him. "That's your mom. You should have said goodbye. I took that away from you."

He leaned in, pressing his body against mine.

"Hey, you did no such thing. This isn't your fault. This was my decision: mine and no one else's. My mom," he paused, "is gone. She knew I loved her and would understand why I didn't go. I truly believe that."

"Yeah, but still—"

"But, nothing. I made my choice, Miracle."

A brief moment of silence lingered between us.

"Can we go say goodbye?" I asked.

"The funeral is over. It was months ago."

"Yeah, but we can still go to her grave site. We can both finally say our goodbyes."

He frowned, wrinkling his forehead.

"Madea would have wanted us to say goodbye, dad."

He sighed and finally gave in.

"Okay, Bubble Gum. Sounds good."

I wrapped my arms around him, squeezing him tighter than ever before.

"But," he started, "I have to make sure the doctor is okay with you taking the trip."

"Okay, that's fine with me."

I let him go from my embrace and he began walking out the door. Before exiting, he turned back and smiled. This smile was genuine and a glint of happiness emerged.

CHAPTER 43

"MAY WE HELP YOU, ma'am?" my dad asked, opening the door wider.

"Clyde?" Her voice was soft and calming.

"Um…yes, I'm Clyde."

I turned to my mom, who shrugged, waiting to see who was at the door. We had only been home for a few hours, so we weren't expecting any company.

The woman took a step inside. My dad allowed it, but he looked apprehensive. When she walked in, my heart sank.

"Madea," I thought.

The woman glided into our apartment. A long red Arkansas shirt flung over her slender frame. A black leather purse with gold beads lining the front hung over her shoulder. I recognized her immediately. It wasn't Madea, but close.

I shot up to my feet and approached the door. She turned to me and the spark in her eyes ignited.

"Hi," I said. My smile was uncontrollable.

"Hi," she said.

We stared at each other for a moment. I could feel my parents' eyes flicking between us.

"Um, I'm sorry, who are you?" my mom asked while standing.

The woman opened her lips, but I cut her off before she could respond.

"Dot Jean."

Again, their eyes flicked between us.

"Dot Jean?" my mom asked.

"Dot Jean?" my dad asked, "Like Madea's Dot Jean?"

I nodded. Dot Jean tilted her head forward, nodding as well.

"Mom. Dad. Do you mind if I speak to her alone, please?"

With a bit of hesitation, they agreed. My dad escorted my mom to the kitchen, sharing a few hushed whispers. I reached out my hand to Dot Jean and led her to the couch.

"When did you wake up?" I asked.

"Oh, it's been about six months or so."

"Six months?" I asked in a whispered tone. "That's about the time we—"

"Yep," she said with a knowing grin.

There was a moment of silence between us. The silence was filled with my mind drowning in questions while I tried to figure out which ones were the best to ask. Then, I tilted my head down, staring at the carpet.

"I'm sorry," I said.

"For what?"

"I didn't save her. I didn't save Kim. She was still attacked; maybe it wouldn't have happened if I had woken up earlier or reached out earlier. I screwed up."

Dot Jean shrugged her shoulders and twisted her face.

"Who is Kim?"

My eyes shot up.

"Kim. Kim," I repeated. I don't know why I thought she would realize who Kim was if I said her name repeatedly. "My best friend who was attacked." I leaned forward, but she just nodded as if she had no idea who I was talking about. "Wait, if it wasn't Kim I was supposed to save, then who was it?"

"When I first saw you, I knew you were like me. You didn't belong in the past. I don't know how I knew; I just did. So, I ran to you. But you're a way faster runner than I ever was," she chuckled.

"Yeah, sorry about that."

"It's okay," she said, smiling. Her body movements were child-like in a way.

"I didn't know if you knew who I was. But I knew my time was running out. If I didn't wake up, I'd never be able to see my family again. To see Texann."

I had to think for a moment before remembering Texann was Madea's real name. People in the South love their nicknames.

"I hoped you would eventually run into me, but today's me. And if you did, I'd hoped you could save me. Didn't know how, but I just knew you'd figure out a way."

My eyes shot up again.

"Wait, save her meant—"

"Save me," she nodded.

I sat back on the couch. This whole time I was to save *Dot Jean* and help *her* wake up.

"So, when I touched you at the hospital—" I asked, not finishing my question.

"I'm pretty sure you woke me up. You saved me." Her head bounced with every word.

"Dang," I said. "Oh, sorry."

"No, dang is a pretty accurate word right now."

We both sat back, letting our memories wash over us.

"How did you wake up?" she asked.

"No clue. I just did."

"But if nothing intervened, then I don't think you're done."

My body tensed.

"What do you mean I'm not done?"

"Well, I don't know for sure, but I'm awake because of you. You intervened for me. So—"

"I could still go back?" Goose bumps spread along my arms at the thought and a hint of nausea rushed over me. "I can't go back. If I do, I don't think…I don't think I'll wake up again."

Her shoulders slumped as her eyes went dull. She didn't respond.

"Hey Dot Jean, would you like to join us for dinner," my mom asked, poking her head out of the kitchen.

Dot Jean turned to me and smiled, "I'd love to."

CHAPTER 44

AT DINNER, DOT JEAN filled us in on her story. She explained how she experienced the same "unknown medical condition" I had when she was little. Thankfully, she didn't go into all the details and kept the whole time-traveling part between us.

I wasn't sure if her story gave my parents hope or increased their concern. Watching me in a "coma" for six months couldn't have been easy, and the possibility of it happening again would scare any parent.

After dessert, Dot Jean told us stories of when she and Madea were younger. My memories of Madea floated from heaven with each story. I wished I had known her when she was younger. She sounded like an amazing teenager.

My parents asked if Dot Jean wanted to spend the night, but she politely declined and only wished we could spend more time together moving forward. Of course, my parents loved that idea. Family was important to them and she was family.

After I walked her to the door, she placed her hand on my chin, cupping it and positioning my face in her direction.

"You're a superhero, young lady. I am blessed to have met you. If I may give you one bit of advice," she said.

I nodded, so she continued.

"Live every day…every second like it's your last because you never know when God will take you away. You hear me?"

"Yes, ma'am," I said.

"Ma'am? It's so weird being old enough to be called ma'am," she said, smiling.

She reached her arms around me, embracing me in a hug. A strange sensation rushed over me. She felt warm yet cold at the same time. Dark and light. Everything and nothing. I closed my eyes and the dark world blasted with images, memories that weren't mine.

I saw her memories. No, I saw her episodes. I went from watching my cousin, Peanut, and his wife give birth to a precious little girl.

Then, I saw a young man stepping on stage. A large hat rested on his head as his long navy-blue gown flowed in the wind. He extended his arm and shook hands with an older woman. Her gown was black and navy blue, with assorted sashes slung over her shoulder.

My heart sank at the next image. It was Dre. Bullet holes pierced his cold flesh while his body leaned against the brick building. His eyes were open, but his vision was empty. A pool of blood served as his floor. I didn't want to see this again. Not today, not ever.

My breathing grew erratic when I continued watching. My mind stumbled back at the sight. Next to my brother's body was the body of a teenage girl. Her braids sprayed across the steps. Her blackish-maroon shirt was riddled with its own bullet holes. Blood leaked from her lips. But unlike Dre, her eyes were closed. She was dead. I was dead.

My body jerked away from Dot Jean. Tears flowed from my eyes. With her hands resting on my shoulders, she stared at me.

"But…How? What?" I stuttered. My words were barely audible between the tears.

"You had to see it. You had to see what I saw." Her words sliced through her tears and she held me tightly. "There was no way I could explain it."

Dot Jean looked like she was in pain. My mind returned to sitting in the hallway with the younger version of her. She once told me maybe we had to change the future. She changed my future.

"I was supposed to—"

"Yes," she said calmly.

"But you saved—"

"Yes." Her words trembled in the still air.

"But…I don't understand."

"We were chosen for a reason, Miracle. I don't know what that reason is, but we both survived. We're both here now. That's all that matters."

I nodded, but I didn't fully understand what she was saying. *She* had survived. *She* made it out of the dream. There was still a good chance I would be pulled back into the darkness. I didn't think I could survive again. I didn't think I would ever wake up again.

After Dot Jean left, I finally realized I couldn't keep all of this bottled up inside me. So, I decided to let someone in on my secret finally. I decided to tell Kim.

CHAPTER 45

We stepped into her room and sat on the edge of her bed. She lowered the volume of her radio, making John Legend's soulful voice barely audible. I scooted to the back of her bed, pressing my back against the wall. She hugged her pink furry pillow and sat cross-legged, waiting for me to talk.

"I need to tell you something. It's a little weird, but hopefully, it'll all make sense in the end. Okay?" I said.

"Okay," she said, eyebrow raised.

I explained everything from my first episode to my last, from Darlene with her angelic voice to Billy, the love-struck young man. I even told her about Dot Jean and the endless white hallway. Everything I knew came to the surface.

Her eyes stayed locked on me as I spoke. Her facial expressions changed with every story. Happiness for the stories about Darlene and sadness for the brown-eyed girl. She rubbed her forehead as if worried through the stories about Billy and almost cried when Dre's name came up.

After I was done, there was a long pause. I allowed all the information to sink into her brain, and I think she did the same. Finally, she spoke.

"Will it happen again?"

"I'm not sure," I paused, "but probably."

Her eyes flickered between me and the carpet.

"Can you visit anyone you want?" she asked.

"No, I think it's just family members. Like I keep returning to Dre and Darlene, who is like my aunt on my mom's side or something like that."

Her hand rubbed her chin as her eyebrows lowered.

"So, Dot Jean…Dot Jean, right?"

"Yes," I said.

"So, Dot Jean saved your life by changing the past?"

"Yes."

She paused for a second, glaring back at the carpet.

"So, what did you change?" she asked. Now, her eyes were locked on mine.

I thought for a moment and responded.

"I'm not sure."

"Oh," she said, somewhat disappointed.

She leaned back against the wall, and I did the same. I didn't know if Kim believed me, but I felt relief knowing I didn't have to keep this secret alone.

Our bodies jumped when the chorus for Taylor Swift's *You Need to Calm Down* blared from Kim's cell phone.

"Hello," she said after lifting the phone to her ear. Her eyebrows twisted as she put on the speaker phone.

"Would you like to accept a collect call from Los Angeles Prison System?" a robotic female voice asked.

She turned to me and I shrugged. With a shaky voice, she responded.

"Yes."

There was a click on the line and then silence.

"Hello?" she asked.

I leaned forward as we both listened to the silence. Heavy breathing slowly crept on the line.

"Hello?" she repeated.

"You know it wasn't me, you lying son of a —"

She hung the phone up quicker than I could react.

"Grrrrrr," she growled, curling her fist and pressing them against her temple. Her phone flew through the air, landing on her pink faux chair.

"Erik?" I asked.

"Yeah, every few weeks, he does this stupid crap. I'll call the police station tomorrow. I wish he would just," she paused, "I wish he would just go away for good."

She sighed, stomping her way to get her phone. I watched every move she made and saw the frustration on her face.

"What was the trial like?" I asked.

She froze. After a few deep, long breaths, she slowly turned and looked at me.

"It was rough." Her words were slow. She stared at me and I stared back. That was all she said. Rough.

I learned later through internet searches that Kim's attack was linked to three others in the neighborhood. Erik was sentenced to nine years, despite having an alibi.

I don't know why Kim didn't tell me that upfront. Maybe comparing her trial with Dre's was too hard for her. Perhaps she felt like she had no business speaking about how hard her trial was when she was the real reason Dre's was so…so rough.

I didn't say anything and neither did she. We just sat on her bed, letting the time slowly creep by.

I left Kim's apartment shortly after. The silence became too unbearable and I felt maybe it was a sign. Plus, it was already dark and I promised my parents I wouldn't be out too late.

As I climbed down her steps, I slid my headphones in and then paused. Going back into the darkness scared me. I already knew music was a trigger, so I put my headphones away and used my surroundings to entertain me.

Stars were splattered across the open sky while small clouds chased each other, flowing with the brisk wind. I tucked my hands into my hoody pocket and watched my steps. The streets were unusually quiet for this time of night, but I didn't mind. Sometimes quiet could be peaceful.

CHAPTER 46

THE QUIET DIDN'T LAST long as music blared ahead of me. I looked up and tilted my head. The passenger door to the vehicle was open as loud music roared out into the night air.

I approached slowly and then my body fell forward, crumbling into a dark existence. My arms reached out as I tried to cling to anything to stop the falling sensation.

"Noooo!" I cried, but it was pointless. My body drifted into the dark abyss and I waited to find out where I would awake.

A long tan sectional couch stretched along the wall as a square coffee table held various opened textbooks. The television blasted Judge Judy, who was busy yelling at a young man complaining about paying child support for three kids.

I turned to see Kim standing in front of the window. Her finger pressed the window blinds down, allowing her to see outside to the street.

"Kim?" I asked.

She couldn't hear me, so I inched closer. I slid my finger between the window blinds and peered out. There was a matte black Chevy Tahoe with blue and red lights flashing and "POLICE" written in giant lettering along the side.

My heart raced as I stumbled backward. My jaw dropped at realizing what I was watching…or was about to watch. I stepped to the window and stared outside.

From this angle, I could see one of the officers leaning out his car window. The other must have still been in the driver's seat. I couldn't hear what he was saying. I didn't need to, though; I knew everything they said.

I saw Dre and a younger me standing on the steps. My heart skipped at the sight of him. My younger self turned to Dre. He looked like a statue, frozen in time.

"Oh my God," Kim mumbled. She released the blinds and dashed to the door. Her hand hovered over the knob for a second, but she didn't turn it. Her hand shook as she let out an audible sigh.

"Open the door," she told herself. "Open. The. Door."

She took a deep breath and then slammed her forehead against the door.

"Dammit," she mumbled.

She turned back to the window and looked out.

By this time, Officer Gladwell was pointing at Dre. He said something to my brother, but Dre didn't respond. I could see the officer step forward. His right hand slowly lowered to his waistband.

"Oh my God," Kim screeched. I stared at her for a moment. She tensed as shaking rummaged over her entire body.

I turned back to the window and lowered the blinds again. My younger self nodded to Dre and then exchanged a few more words between them and us. Officer Gladwell motioned for us to go upstairs and we did. My heart exploded at what was about to happen.

Kim's breathing calmed as we walked up the stairs. "Gun!"

The shout was deafening. Officer Gladwell drew his gun, crouched down, and aimed his pistol at my brother. Dre's hands flew to the sky. His fingers stretched out. I couldn't see his face since his back was to me, but I remembered the fear in his eyes. It was those eyes that haunted me at night, still.

The officer began yelling at Dre, who slowly reached his arm around his back. It was too low to see, but I knew what he was grabbing.

I didn't want to turn away, but Kim's breathing grew loud, erratic. I turned to her. Her eyes swelled and her chin quivered. I positioned myself right next to her. She couldn't see me, but she still needed me there.

The officers' screams brought my eyes back to the window.

"Lower the weapon slowly!"

"Get down, now! Do you hear me? Now!"

Suddenly, Dre's body disappeared from our vantage point. Then, he reappeared. His body jerked to the side. He lowered to a crouching position, gun in hand. His bent body appeared like his eyes were lining up with the gun.

"No," I said, "he slipped. This isn't right. He—"

Before I could finish my thought, the blast of the officer's gun pierced through the air. My heart shattered with every squeeze of the trigger. I pushed myself away from the window. And then I saw it.

Kim had the same reaction. Her hand flung to her chest as her body curled over. Tears streamed down her cheeks. She screamed out. Her voice sounded like an injured wild animal.

"Noooo!" she cried.

The last bang made the Earth go quiet. I stared at Kim but could no longer hear her screams. Everything went silent.

The darkness slowly blanketed the light and I was again flushed into the dark abyss. My body fell through the non-existent world as my mind traversed between thoughts.

Greg's words repeated in my brain, "Kim saw what she saw." I didn't want to believe it, but from where she was standing, it looked like Dre…it looked like Dre was pointing the gun at the officers.

CHAPTER 47

I GASPED FOR AIR, thankful to be awake once more. The beat-up brown truck idled in front of me as the world came alive again. I lowered my head to peer inside. Empty. My heart began to race as the situation seemed too familiar.

Behind me, a figure emerged from the darkness. I slowly turned and my heart sank. Shadows partially hid his face, but his square chin stretched out into the light while his menacing eyes peered into my inner being.

As he stepped forward, his face became more visible. It was Erik. No, it was Kurt, his older brother.

They both had slim builds, but Kurt was more muscular and had an extra few inches on his younger brother. When he stepped into the light, a sandy crew cut outlined his head, with an unimpressive fu-mancho finishing his look.

"What do you want?" I asked. I stared at his hands. No weapon in sight. But his brother always carried a butterfly knife. I assumed his weapon of choice ran in the family.

"You're the one who got my brother locked up, huh?" Although it was a question, it sounded more like a statement—an accusative statement at that.

"Your brother is the one who got himself locked up," I said, slowly backing up. I slid my hand inside my pocket, reaching for my keys.

His lips stretched from one ear to the other. He lowered his head and lurched forward, wrapping his hands around my shoulders. The moon's light reflected against his eyes, revealing the monster beneath his flesh.

I slid my hand out of my pocket, jabbing forward, driving the key into his neck. He jumped back but didn't let go. My right hand slammed against his eye. A stinging sensation rattled my bones on impact.

His left hand flew through the air, nailing me on the side of my head, buckling my knees. The ringing was instant. My keys dropped to the ground and I was on the pavement before I knew what hit me.

He straddled me, pinning me to the ground. My arms stretched out, blocking him from putting his entire weight on me. But his strength was too much. His fist smashed against my cheek, flinging my teeth to the ground.

Another fist collided with my temple, bells pounding in my head. I screamed out. He leaned back and chuckled. He was having fun.

Tears ran down my cheek as my screams floated to the star-lit sky.

"Stupid little girl," he snickered.

My chest sank as he pressed his weight on top of me. An elbow flew through the air. I covered up as best I could. But, even when I blocked, the impact did damage with every hit.

"Not so tough now, huh?" he screamed. He leaned back again to admire his work.

Taking advantage of his distraction, my hands crashed into his face. My thumbs dug into his eyes, and I squeezed. Something tore as blood oozed out, leaking onto my chest. He let out a blood-curdling scream.

"Ahhh," he shrieked.

As he wrenched back in pain, I propped onto my elbows and pushed my body back. I only needed a few inches. I shot my knees back and drove deep and hard into his chest.

He jerked back. It wasn't far, but it was enough for me to stagger to my feet and run.

"Fire! Fire," I screamed.

I didn't look back, but I swear I felt his breath on my neck. I ran as hard as I could, screaming the entire time.

CHAPTER 48

THREE POLICE CARS WERE blocking half the street as red and blue lights flashed in the air. A male officer, maybe in his late 20s, asked me questions and I answered them. Then, a more senior officer came over and I repeated my answers to him.

With each question, my mind dove back into the attack: his cold fingers gripping my skin, his snake-like eyes peering into my soul, and his arrogant laugh as he admired his brutality. The monster!

The police escorted me back to the Lancaster Police Station.

"Have a seat here and we'll find you an empty room," Officer Sanchez said, motioning to the chair. "Need anything to drink or eat?"

My head twisted back and forth as I sat and pressed an ice pack on my battered face.

"Okay, if you need anything, let me know. Your parents should be here soon. I'll be right there if you need anything." She pointed to a desk and then slowly walked away.

My mind flipped between memories of the attack and the present. It felt unreal, like I was living in a movie scene. But, in movies, the attack victim bounces back in a few hours after pointing to their attacker in a line-up. After a hot shower and some strong coffee, they live perfectly everyday lives.

Reality, however, was a stark contrast. I felt like I didn't want to go on living. Like no part of me could bounce back, no matter how strong the coffee or hot the shower was. And I didn't want to see Kurt again, not even in a line-up.

But deep down, I knew I had to. Plus, the fighter in me didn't give up before and wasn't going to give up now. I told myself I had to keep fighting. I had to keep pressing forward.

The physical injuries would heal…eventually. It was my mental scars that worried me. There was a fear within me of them intertwining with my shadow, never truly leaving my side. But they would not break me. Kurt did not break me.

"Breathe," I told myself, "just breathe!"

My chest expanded as air rushed into my lungs. I closed my eyes and focused on my breathing. The veil of darkness blanketed the world as eerie silence brushed over my thoughts. I released another deep breath and peeled my hands from over my eyes, and the world slowly regained focus.

The End

WAIT!!!

Thank you for taking the time to read my book. It is because of the fans that this book even exists, so thank you. If you enjoyed it, please leave a review wherever you purchased the book. Every review helps me improve my writing.

Signed,
Your faithful author,
Rodney LaMarr

For more information on my upcoming projects, please visit my website at: www.rodneylamarr.com.

www.ingramcontent.com/pod-product-compliance
Lightning Source LLC
Chambersburg PA
CBHW031535310726
48971CB00008B/2491